Foodies Rush In

By

Tanya Eby

ALSO BY TANYA EBY

Easy Does It

Blunder Woman

Pepper Wellington And The Case of the Missing Sausage

Eby Ink LLC
PO Box 68872
Grand Rapids, MI 49516

First Printing: June 2012

ISBN- 978-0-9860133-0-0

Cover design by Alysia Hough

Visit the author's website www.TanyaEby.com

For David,

For making me believe

that true love is possible

Foodies Rush In

Chapter 1

Even before Dana set her bags on the wooden floor of her 1950s era cookie cutter house, she could hear her kids calling her name and running over themselves to get to her.

"Mommy! Mommy!" they cried. Were there two more beautiful words in the English language? Maybe "Eat Chocolate" but "Mommy! Mommy!" came a close second.

She set her bags down, kneeled, opened her arms and was promptly tackled by her four-year-old daughter dressed in layers of pink tulle, and her six-year-old son dressed as a zombie. "I thought Halloween was over. It's supposed to be Thanksgiving soon!" she said amidst the kisses and elbows and general head butting that represented the love-fest greeting from her kids.

"Don't you know?" she heard her sister Valerie say. "They're not dressed up. This is how they *are*, like all the time."

Dana peeled her daughter Ruby from her neck, and lifted her son Zach off her stomach and sat up. "Should I have warned you before I left?" she asked.

Her sister smiled. "To tell you the truth, I sorta already knew. Come on kiddos, give your mom some space to settle in before you maul her to death. You'd think she'd been gone for a year and not just five days."

"Hey! Mom. Mom. Mom. Mom? Mom," Ruby chanted. "Ma? Mommy. Mom. Hey. Mom."

Dana shook her head and smiled. "What, sweetie?"

"You bring me something?" Ruby shot her that smile that melted icebergs.

Her son stared at her intently. For a brief moment Dana thought he was going to ask her for brains—it must've been the makeup. Instead, he said, "What I'd really like is some more Clone Troopers. They have any Clone Troopers in Vegas?"

"Not exactly. But they did have these." Dana pulled two plastic jars of M&Ms from her bag. She'd had them printed with the kids' names on them. She had tons of swag from the conference, but most of it related to her new canning venture and was being shipped to her. The t-shirts, mugs, necklaces, and small velvet painting of Elvis for her sister, waited in her bag.

The kids grabbed the M&Ms and scampered off to sort colors and devour the candy mercilessly.

Valerie stared at her, arms crossed over her gigantic boobs—thanks to lactating for twins. Dana gave her sister some credit. She at least waited until the kids were out of earshot before she said, "Okay, dish. Who's the guy and are you pregnant?"

"No, I'm not pregnant! Don't be ridiculous! We didn't even…" Dana lowered her voice to a whisper, "sleep together."

"You're not supposed to sleep. That's not how I got pregnant. I sure as heck wasn't sleeping."

"It was nothing," Dana said, trying to sound as if it really was nothing. She scooped up her bag, opened it and handed her sister the 5x7 portrait of Elvis. When you put him on the wall and walked back and forth in front of him, his eyes seemed to follow you everywhere. It was creepy, yet comforting at the same time.

"Oh, no," Valerie said. "You are not distracting me with artistic genius. I want his name, his height, his income level, and when are you seeing him again."

"Theodore Drimmel." Dana waited to see her sister's reaction. It took Valerie a moment to think it over and then her nose crinkled as if she smelled something bad.

"I like the Theodore part," she said, "but that *Drimmel* has got to go. Maybe he can take your name when you get married."

"Valerie! Don't be ridiculous. It was a fling. I'm not going to…" Suddenly, Dana saw herself standing next to a punked-out Theo and both of them giggling, right after they'd said "I do" and "Oy".

Dana continued, "Look, do you want the vital statistics or not? I can give you age, height, and income level, but not much else. And…is there any coffee? I'm in need of a serious jolt of caffeine. I know it was only five days, but there's a three hour time difference."

Valerie nodded and walked into Dana's kitchen. Dana loved her kitchen. Sure, it could be a little bigger, but it had all the earth tones she loved. Green cabinets, creamy brown counters flecked with golds and greens, easy-to-clean linoleum. It hardly sounded romantic, but when her then-husband Paul had said she could do anything she wanted to the kitchen—within a budget—she'd thought she'd won a trip to France. Of course, she realized he'd given her free reign of the kitchen around the same time he'd started seeing his new wife. Best not to think about that.

Valerie grabbed two mugs, poured equal amounts of cream into both and topped it off with hazelnut coffee. "Yes," she said before Dana could question her. "I'm back to drinking caffeine. The twins aren't sleeping through the night yet, so that means I'm pretty much constantly wired. His name is Theodore," she transitioned from one thought to the next so quickly that Dana had trouble noticing they were on two different subjects.

"Yes. And he's opening a gourmet food store somewhere in the Midwest, so he's employed and gets some kind of paycheck. He paid for things for me without hesitation, and I haven't experienced that since…well, never. He's a few inches taller than me, so I can still wear heels. He's nice. Funny. Cute in a TV CSI scientist kind of way. What else? He's a great kisser. But that's all I know. Nothing else."

"You forgot to say when you're seeing each other again."

"We're not. Ever." Dana sipped her coffee, reveling the warmth it gave her, and then became aware that the warmth was actually from the glare her sister was giving her. "Don't give me that look, Val. It's not a big deal. It's a small deal. A good deal actually. It's ridiculous to even think that I'd see him again. I'm a mom. I'm busy. I haven't dated since The Culture Club was considered edgy. And everyone says what happens in Vegas stays in Vegas."

"Yeah…well, everyone is stupid. Are stupid. Everyone are stupid." Valerie looked confused. "Seriously. I have baby momma brain. Don't listen to everyone is what I'm trying to say."

"I'm not ready to date."

"Yes, you are."

"No, I'm not."

Valerie set her mug down on the countertop. They listened to the kids shouting out random colors. Zach was trying to trade Ruby one blue for four purple and Ruby wasn't allowing it. Smart girl, Dana thought.

Valerie yelled at the top of her lungs "Knock it off, kiddos, or you'll wake the twins!" then immediately said, "Paul's been gone a year. You've been divorced since June. The holidays are breathing down your neck. You. Are. Ready. To. Date." Then she sipped her coffee in an "enough said" sort of way.

Dana felt the familiar plum rise in her throat any time she thought of her ex. It was true that she'd been devastated when he left, but honestly, she wasn't shocked. They weren't right for each other. They liked each other, married each other because they'd thought the other one was "good enough". Truthfully, they'd both had biological clocks that were not only ticking, but booming. And they'd had five years together. Five years of coexisting together, but not really living. Not fully. So when he'd met and fallen in love with someone else—Dana had been devastated and hurt, but not at all surprised. And she'd never seen Paul happier.

That might've been what hurt the most. That and Paul seemed content to see the kids only occasionally, especially now that Alyssa was expecting.

Dana had tried to imagine herself going out on dates again. How did one do that? Dating was a horrible experience in her twenties. She couldn't imagine doing it now in her late thirties, with two kids. And what would she do? How would she even approach the topic of who she was and what she offered now? She could just imagine walking up to an attractive man and saying, "Hey, I'm Dana! I'm a single mom with two kids. Do you want to be an instant dad? Do you want to have frenzied sex when the kids are at their dad's and secret sex once every month while the kids are sleeping? Because that's probably what we'll do. Oh! And are you willing to go through a police check and probably an anal probe just to make sure you're not hiding anything, because I've watched a lot of America's Most Wanted over the years, and I am not letting any freaks near my children."

Dana had a few issues.

"I'm not ready to date, Val," she said, this time using her End of Discussion tone. "Besides," she finished, "he's already married." She just didn't say that technically, if you didn't think of paperwork, he was married to *her*.

Chapter 2

Theodore thinly sliced his already thinly sliced piccata. He sliced it into strips and then across the grain. The slicing was so delicate and impressive it was a shame he didn't record it and post in on YouTube. Finally, he speared the chicken with his fork, swirled it in the lemon caper sauce and then took a bite. It melted. It really melted in his mouth! He tried to enjoy it, but he felt awful.

Sarah sat across from him in the dining room, a simple room really with a sturdy 1950s era table on it. Sarah hated the table, but Theodore liked its usefulness, especially when he made pasta. Tonight though, they'd covered the metal table with a dark linen, and Sarah had insisted on candlelight. Theodore wasn't sure why, exactly. He was the only one eating, hardly a romantic dinner when only one of the two was actually enjoying a meal. It was sort of like dancing a waltz by yourself and that was uncomfortable, even if you didn't step on anyone's toes.

She had declined the dinner he'd prepared and even the peanut butter and jelly sandwich. She leaned forward, the buttons on her blue cardigan sweater sparkling in the candlelight. She was wearing a blue wool skirt with matching blue shoes. Her legs were crossed daintily under the table. Theodore was in awe of all that matching. It seemed sort of unnatural. Monstrous even.

"And then I called the caterer and I was like 'Uh, excuse me? We are NOT eating raw meat at MY wedding. I don't care if you call it Carpaccio or whatever.' I totally said that. What I should of said is that foreign names cover up the true meaning of what something is. I mean, if Carpaccio means raw ass beef but sliced thin, then call it Raw Ass Beef. Or maybe Raw Beef Ass. Yeah. Call it Raw Beef Ass and put it on a piece of toast and not a fucking broosketia or whatever."

"Bruschetta," Theodore said softly, and then took another bite of his foreign named dinner that was, in his opinion, absolutely divine.

"Whatever. There's no way we're having that. I want stuffed chicken or steak and asparagus and mashed potatoes. Doesn't that sound delicious? Oh, I could just die and eat it all right now, but then I wouldn't fit in my dress. And you want me to fit in my dress, don't you, so that then you could…take…it…off." Sarah used her matching shoe to trace circles on Theodore's pant leg. It rather hurt. For just an instant, he remembered sitting across from Dana at Excalibur as she ate a turkey leg that was so enormous it blocked out her face.

"Look, Sarah," he said with a little more force than he'd intended. In fact, he hadn't intended to say anything, but his mouth seemed to have a mind of its own. "I've done something. I have to tell you. I…it's Vegas."

She said nothing for a moment. Her breathing made the candle flame flicker. "I don't want to know. It stays in Vegas, okay?"

"It isn't okay. It's not okay. How could I…?" he paused, his appetite leaving him entirely. What he wanted to say was how could he kiss another woman? How could he even joke at marrying another woman? How was he supposed to marry this woman when he was fantasizing about a woman whom he knew only a few things about: her name, that she made jams, and that she had the best sense of humor he'd ever encountered. Not to mention a great pair of legs. And her clothes never matched. And she smelled like brown sugar. What he said instead was, "I'm a pig, Sarah."

Sarah pursed her lips. "I know that. Just shut up about it. I want to plan our wedding. It will be perfect."

To Theodore, it rather sounded like a threat.

And then it occurred to him. Maybe he couldn't even marry Sarah. Oh, he wanted to all right. Sure! This was what they'd decided. He wanted to settle down and get married, and Sarah wanted him to settle down and get married. Although, really, he was pretty much already settled. If he were being honest with himself, he'd say he wanted to get unsettled.

He took another bite of his piccata. How different would dinner be if he actually had someone with him to enjoy it? Sure Sarah was there, but they weren't really together. Then it occurred to him. The idea. And he understood why someone coined the phrase "an idea dawned" because it did feel, indeed, like a dawning within him. He felt like he actually glowed. He couldn't marry Sarah! No! Not until he knew if that phony little ceremony they'd played at in Vegas might actually mean something. Could it be…was it possible…that he was already married?

He remembered standing next to Dana, their fingers laced together. She looked ridiculous with her hair sprayed so large that she had to turn sideways to walk through doors. They were drunk and giggling and then when Elvis—Elvis!—had asked them to say their vows, they hadn't hesitated. Thinking of this, Theodore realized that he could barely even tell Sarah he'd see her tomorrow. It made him feel like a terrible person.

"I had no idea there were so many different kinds of napkins. I mean there's white and cream and eggshell and butter and I was like, look, I'm paying you tons of money for something people are just going to wipe their mouths on anyway so why don't *you* do the work and fucking choose the color yourself. Then we decided on butter. It's slightly creamier than the eggshell." Sarah continued to talk at him and Theodore ate until his plate was clean. She didn't want to discuss Las Vegas with him. In fact, it was almost like she was pretending that he hadn't even begun a discussion on his actions there.

He understood that it might be painful for her and she had so many things on her mind, but that didn't mean he was going to sit and be quiet. No. He felt, somehow, that he'd need to tell her eventually. You couldn't marry someone you had secrets from, could you? Should you?

Theodore finished his chicken. The dawning of an idea left him and he realized that though he was full from his dinner, there was still something in him that was very much empty.

Chapter 3

Dana was finally over her jet lag. It seemed ridiculous to even say she had jet lag when the plane ride had only been a few hours, and her whole adventure lasted a mere five days. Maybe then, what she suffered from was Adventure Lag. Las Vegas represented the first really exciting thing she'd done since giving birth, and she wasn't all that certain she should count giving birth as an adventure really. Giving birth was…an act of alchemy. Something surely only sorcerers could do. It was magical and the pain had been so intense that all she could do was ride it out, the way one endures a roller coaster ride when they were terrified of heights. And Dana had done that little adventure. Twice.

Las Vegas was another kind of adventure. One in which she hadn't felt like Dana the Mom, Dana the Sister, Dana the Now Divorced, Dana the Lactating Cow—thankfully she was done with lactating—or Dana the Adjunct Instructor. No, she'd been Dana the Entrepreneur, Dana the

Owner of Dana's Delights. And then later, in the wedding chapel, in the elevator pressed up against the wall with Theo's hands in her hair, his lips against her neck, she ceased to be even that and had become, miraculously, Dana the Woman.

Dana the Woman. Who knew that underneath her sweater and slacks, there lurked an actual living and breathing woman, a sexual being, and not just a mom, sister, teacher, friend?

It was nice to be reminded of it—which was why on her return to teaching, she did something a little different. Instead of wearing her armor-like bra and underwear so supportive it could've run a therapy group, she opted for a light grey lacy bra and matching panty. Why? Because after she dropped the kids off at daycare and preschool and as she walked into her office at the community college, she felt just a little bit naughty. She didn't need to feel naughty for anyone in particular. It was nice to feel naughty just with herself. And in the future, she'd probably have a romantic relationship just with herself. That was her reality, and she was okay with that. At least when you were romancing yourself, you were certain to be satisfied.

"You're smiling," Jennie Koepp, another adjunct said to her. Jennie was twenty-five with breasts so perky they seemed eternally optimistic. She was also incredibly cute. She was the short, curly redheaded kind of person that made you think immediately of Anne of Green Gables or Pippi Longstocking, except without the history of being neglected and abandoned. To top it off, she was from Canada and had that adorable accent thing where her O's sounded strangely rounded and comforting. "Oh! Was Las Vegas just amazing? Did you have just the best time? You did? Didn't you? Did you get married? Where's the ring?"

Dana's heart stopped. Was Jennie a psychic along with being an optimist? Could those two things possibly fit together? Then she realized that Jennie was joking.

Dana sat at her desk. Adjuncts shared an office, and there were six or so of them using this one on a rotating basis. Dana taught rhetoric classes to freshmen and prepared them for adulthood by teaching them how to write a really interesting essay. Jennie, on the other hand, taught a class in archaeology and occasionally one on abnormal psychology. She was every incoming male freshman's dream woman, and quite possibly some of the female's, too.

"No ring," Dana said and then laughed. "But I did bring you some chocolate." She tossed Jennie a bar.

"Mmm." Jennie opened it and immediately began to eat. She talked between mouthfuls. "What I'd really like though is some of your jams. Are you taking orders yet? In honor of Brent's heritage, we're going to celebrate Thanksgiving, and I'm having all his family and my family over."

"Don't you celebrate Thanksgiving in Canada?" Dana asked.

"Oh, yeah. Sure we do. Only it's in October and not November. That's really the only difference. We eat all the same food and stuff, only instead of being grateful and all that for being Americans, we're grateful we're Canadians. But this year, I wanted to celebrate *your* Thanksgiving too. So I'm doing another turkey dinner and stuffing and all that, and I wanted your jams for some goodie bags. Something Michigan-y. Maybe with cherries in it. And I'll totally buy it because I told my mom I was doing this, and she's already deposited money into the account. The Canadian dollar is worth almost more than the U.S. now. She was proud of that."

With that, Jennie wiped her mouth on a tissue and discarded the empty wrapper. "So? Are you ready for orders yet?"

Dana smiled to herself. The whole point for her in going to the food entrepreneur conference in Las Vegas in the first place was the crazy idea that she should get as much information as possible so she could start selling her jams, chutneys, jellies and whatever else she decided to make. She wanted to take orders. Usually, she just gave away all the food she prepared, but with her single income and no real idea whether or not the school was going to hire her next semester, she needed something to fall back on. It was hard to sell to her friends, but she knew they wanted to help. Even if Jennie were just being nice, Dana didn't care. It was the sweetest offer.

She grabbed her pen and said, "Well. Okay. I could do a cherry chutney, which is great with pork or turkey. Or I still have blueberry jam from this summer. Oh! And this peach preserve that is so delicious it's like canned sunshine." Dana paused. "That's incredibly corny. I can't believe I just said that."

Jennie shook her head. "No! Are you kidding? That's just what my side of the family needs. Some canned sunshine. It's super cloudy in Ottawa. What are they? Six each?"

Dana nodded her head. It was so hard to charge for what she loved making, but good ingredients were expensive and at six dollars a jar, she'd make a nice little profit.

"Sweet!" Jennie said. "Why don't you just give me, oh, thirty or so?"

Dana gasped. "What?"

"Yeah. Brent's parents divorced and then got remarried and then divorced and remarried again. I'm inviting everyone. It's going to be a real American Thanksgiving complete with talk-show type awkwardness and potential violence between family members. I'm so excited. So. Yeah. Thirty?"

Dana nodded. She opened her computer and the empty spreadsheet she'd created last night on what she thought was a flight of whimsy. Then she began entering in Jennie's order. It occurred to her as she typed that Dana Kupiac was now Owner of Dana's Delight as well as Wearer of Sexy Underwear. Somehow, she was actually in business.

Chapter 4

Downtown Grand Rapids was really a booming little place, Theodore thought. This year's ArtPrize — a massive art celebration/competition — had wrapped up last month, in which the entire downtown area was turned into a modern art museum…or a wax house of horror depending on your perspective. Either way, the downtown had been crawling with tourists and families and business people all looking to crown the next winning art piece. There were great restaurants in town and music, and now even a growing film industry.

This burgeoning downtown came as a surprise to most people, and especially to Theodore. When he'd gone to high school, downtown Grand Rapids had been more a place for punk runaways to congregate. So, five years ago, when he and his business partner Mike opened their first gourmet food store, they did so in the suburbs of Detroit, thinking that the city would recover eventually. The city hadn't exactly recovered. It was going through an identity crisis really, but the store had done fine. They'd stocked it with great wines and imported cheeses, a deli case filled with delicacies as well as pasta salad, and desserts so sinful one could actually earn points to go to hell by simply eating one truffle.

Mike ran the Detroit business, and business was going so well they'd decided to invest in another store. Because Theodore had relocated to Grand Rapids to settle down with his fiancée Sarah and be closer to her family, they'd decided to open the next store right in the heart of the city, in the Monroe Center.

Monroe Center was a strip about two blocks long that featured the Grand Rapids Art Museum and Rosa Parks Circle, an area where concerts and rallies were held outside the art museum and in the winter an ice skating rink was put up. Trees lined the streets and were sprinkled with tiny lights from November until February. There were restaurants, bars, a local bookstore, dress shops and an atmosphere that was both urban and somehow family-friendly. Theodore loved it. Sarah, on the other hand, was terrified of being in Downtown, where she shivered if she came within a few feet of anyone who looked like they might be either homeless or a college student—she was terrified of both. Sarah liked the comfort of more suburban, safely Christian areas like Jenison and Rockford.

The new store was called "Foodies". Theodore liked the name. It was simple, yet gave a customer an immediate feel for the place. Their store in Detroit was called "The Grape and Fig" and was classy and had classical music, and ultimately it bored Theodore just a little bit. He wanted this new store to be a little more friendly, a little more inviting, and have a little more sense of humor. It was one of the reasons he'd gone to Las Vegas. He wanted to feature the typical gourmet fare that people picked up to impress dinner parties, but he also wanted something more. He wanted food that was interesting, fanciful. He wanted his store to be a reflection of the person he'd always wanted to be, but somehow wasn't. At least not yet.

"Over there," he said and directed the movers on where they were going to set up the shelving unit. They had one week to get everything up and running. He'd wanted to open before Thanksgiving.

Outside, lights twinkled on the trees. A soft snow was falling, one of the first of the season. It was rather more of a practice snow, the way it danced through the wind. For a moment he watched the builders put the shelving unit together, listened to the drill whir, and then something outside the window caught his eye. A woman with dark brown hair and a bright red coat walked by. Was that…? Could that be…? It wasn't possible. No. But maybe…

"Hey! Where are you going?" cried his partner Mike, who was helping the construction workers by holding two parts of the shelving unit together. In jeans and a T-shirt, he was actually dressed for helping, whereas Theodore was more dressed for tax season.

"Something important just happened," Theodore said, even before he had a chance to think. And then he was out the door, without his jacket, and running down the streets of Monroe Center, calling out the one word he'd thought he'd never say again, "Dana!"

He was running down the street, suit jacket and tie flapping. If there'd been more wind, Theodore might've lifted off and become the very first human kite. When he'd finally caught up to her in front of Tre Cugini, he cried "Dana!" one last time and then reached for her shoulder. He should've realized something was off when he reached up to touch her shoulder and not down.

The woman screamed. And then she slapped him. "My name isn't Dana, mutherfucker; it's Angelique, so you better just back away. And if you want my purse or something, then you're going to have to fight me for it. I know karate and I will use every ounce of my chi or whatever and kick your balls so hard they fly up your throat."

The woman, as Theodore could plainly see now, didn't even resemble Dana in the slightest, except for the brown hair. This woman was tall. Massive almost. And black. What could he do? "I'm so sorry," he said and held up his palms in an effort to show he wasn't hiding any weapons.

"Yeah, you better be. And you better just back away real slowly. That's right, mutherfucker. I watch Tarantino movies and I will take you down." She eyed him suspiciously.

"Really. Huge mistake. Embarrassing mistake." He took two more steps backwards and then it occurred to him he might have something to fix this. "Listen, do you like wine?"

The woman crossed her arms over her chest. "Are you asking me out?"

Theodore gulped. "No! No. I'm engaged actually. I run a store that's opening next week…up the block…here's a coupon for a free bottle of wine. Just come in any time and I'll help you pick one out." He took a business card from his wallet and scribbled a note on the back then placed the card down on the sidewalk, as one would a fully-loaded weapon.

"Apologies," he said, and then turned and speed-walked back to Foodies…but not before he heard the woman call after him, "Your fiancée's name better be Dana or you have some explaining to do to that woman!"

Chapter 5

It was cold outside. Dana pulled the belt of her red coat tighter, but it did little to warm her. It was time to put away the fall clothes and bring out the winter ones. She'd thought she could wait until at least after Thanksgiving. On second thought, she reminded herself, this was Michigan. West Michigan. Where cold drifted from Chicago, danced with the precipitation over Lake Michigan, and then dumped massive blankets of snow on her city for five months of the year. Dana didn't mind. She'd rather be cold and snuggling with someone for warmth then sitting outside in the humidity of July and August. Although, maybe it was just the snuggling part she liked. She shook her head. That was long gone now. If she wanted to snuggle, she had two adorable kids who'd do so willingly for at least ten seconds each, if she paid them.

Dana shifted the bag on her shoulder. Her bags were always packed with too much stuff. Today, it contained her computer, papers to grade at night, lipstick, wallet, mini hairspray to prevent Crazy Cat Lady hair from forming, and two jars of her preserves. She'd passed by "Foodies" numberless times on her way to work. And the sign said they'd be opening next week. Selling thirty or so jars to Jennie had given her just that little boost of extra confidence she needed. A friend would buy one or two jars to be nice. But not thirty. Jennie obviously liked her product. And if there was one thing Dana had learned in Las Vegas—besides kissing in an elevator even at age thirty-seven, was extremely hot—she'd learned that successful business people believe in their business.

Dana knocked and the door opened; she felt her breath leave her body. In front of her were three very handsome men, bent over and building stuff. For a moment, she saw one of the men draw a hand across his sweaty brow. Sawdust floated in the air like confetti. Another man bent to pick up a large piece of wood and his muscles flexed. It was like walking into some erotica novel; one of them just needed to be dressed like a pirate—or perhaps a mechanic. A pirate who also fixed cars.

Dana almost giggled watching the man hold his wood. *He's holding his wood*, she thought, and was glad she had at least some control as to not say it out loud.

The words "Can I help you?" shook her from her nearly X-rated moment. She'd just been about to imagine fans blowing the construction workers' hair, their bare torsos glistening with perspiration, her lips parting to…

Dana blinked. Then she blinked again just to re-focus. "Hi, there. I'm Dana Kupiac owner of Dana's Delights." She held out her hand and the man in jeans and a t-shirt shook it.

"Mike Sparrow, co-owner of Foodies." He smiled at her, and she was struck suddenly by an instant awareness of energy roiling in the room between them. At any moment, David Attenborough was going to narrate their exchange with, "Look at how the female's pupils have dilated. That is a sure sign that she is physically attracted to the male, perhaps even willing to mate."

"Uh…" She swallowed. Either she needed medication or she needed a romance novel, a bottle of wine, and some time alone in the bathroom. And STAT. If she could only say something, then maybe she could blow out the flame of her overactive imagination. *Don't say 'blow'. Don't say 'blow'.* She repeated inwardly. Luckily, outwardly she said, "I can see you're really busy. I have a small business. Start-up really…and I just wanted to drop off two samples for you. Here's Raspberry Ribbon. It's terrific on toast or over goat cheese with crackers. And I have a spiced apple chutney, also good as an appetizer, but terrific with turkey. And I'm a local business so you could…uh…highlight the whole shop local thing…"

Mike nodded. "We'll take a case of each. How does that sound?"

Dana had to shake her head just to make sure she was hearing correctly. "You're kidding, right?"

He looked around as if actually searching for the punch line. "No. My partner and I like to support local businesses. I'll set up a little trial area for customers, probably with cheese and crackers. We'll see how these two cases go, twenty-four jars, yes? And then after that we can talk more." While Dana listened to him, she could almost see him in a low-cut polyester shirt with chest hair and gold chains. This man had Player written all over him. Maybe even literally. Still, there was something so masculine about him he sort of made her want to reveal her lacy grey…

Dana couldn't breathe. Then she did breathe and said, "But you haven't even tried them yet. These could be absolutely horrible. You don't even know me! I could've stolen these from somewhere and been riding around in a van trying to sell them to unsuspecting customers."

He laughed. "Are they horrible? Are they stolen? Do you even have a van?"

Dana didn't even need to think about it. "No and no, but I do have a minivan. Actually, the jams, they're terrific."

"Then we have a deal." He extended his hand again and they shook...for what seemed to Dana a rather extended time. He stared at her intently, the way a lion might stare at a gazelle before claiming it for dinner.

"Okay, then. I'll just leave these two for you and...oh...my card." She withdrew her warm hand from his in the hopes she'd done so before she broke out into a cool sweat. She'd actually taken a glance at his lower half. At his jeans. At the slight swell in the front of his jeans. She needed to get out of Foodies before she spontaneously combusted and/or David Attenborough returned to narrate her mating ritual, "And so we see the female extend her hind quarters to the male..."

Dana reached into her cavernous bag, grabbed a handful of cards and thrust them at him. A few dropped to the ground. "Sorry!" she said. "Sorry!" and then bent to pick them up.

He bent with her. "No worries," he said and then looked at her again. "I think things are going to be just fine. I have a good feeling about this."

Did he lick his lips, Dana thought. He did! He did!

Dana handed him the last of the cards. She tried not to analyze just what he had meant about "feelings" and "this". "Okay, then," she said. "Nice to meet you." He stood and for a brief moment, on her knees, Dana stared right at his crotch. And then she screamed a little bit. She really did.

She jumped to her feet, turned around, and fled, the door jingling behind her.

"See you soon!" he called after her.

Dana hunkered herself into the collar of her coat and walked briskly to her car. *Just focus, Dana, focus* she told herself…but in her mind, oh, in her mind she was absolutely primal, inspired no doubt by the very masculine and slightly scary Mike Sparrow. She didn't envision being primal with him; that would take more energy than she could spend. Instead, she was back in Vegas with Theo and they were kissing, only in her mind, this time they were naked.

It made for a rather awkward fantasy since she still had them in the elevator, but tonight when the kids were safely asleep in bed, she could tweak the dream. She'd imagine satin sheets, Las Vegas lights blinking around, and Theo's pants slowly unzipping with the help of her teeth.

Good God, she thought. It was going to be a long fifty or so years on her own. She'd thought at thirty-seven, divorced, a single mom, that she'd lost all ability to feel even the slightest bit of sexual *anything*. Boy, had she been wrong. In her mind, David Attenborough agreed by saying, "You go, girl."

Chapter 6

Mike Sparrow laughed to himself. He'd just bought a case of jam without even trying it, and all because of a pretty woman. His soon-to-be-ex-wife was right; he just couldn't get enough of a pretty face. Or a pretty pair of lips. Or a nice rack. That Dana Delight woman had all of it, and probably more. He could use a little Delight right now, especially from a brunette.

He sighed. It would be so easy to run after her, take her soft hand in his, say a couple of lines to her, and then have her naked in his bed sometime in the evening. He was a pro at getting women into his bed. He was also a pro at marrying them. So, no. As cute and perky as she'd looked, he was not going to run after her. He'd ignore the sexual chemistry he'd felt popping between them, and he'd return to his work. Work right now was getting Foodies up and running, and then getting his life up and running.

His third marriage was beyond help for getting back on track. No, he'd pretty much destroyed every oath he'd taken, and Michelle—finding him in bed with their next door neighbor—really hadn't helped any. No. That little spontaneous action had cost him more than he cared to think about. Michelle had opened the door, saw them going at it, and then quietly slipped down the stairs, went straight to the bank, emptied their account, and then filed for divorce…after kicking him out of their house in the Detroit suburbs.

So the universe had granted him yet another chance at starting over. Only unlike with his first two wives, this time, he was starting over with virtually nothing. That was why he had to focus on the business. And that meant no more Dana Delights, or Beatrice Delights, or cute College Girl Delights. Delight was out. Work was in.

He helped the construction guys install the last of the shelving. Nothing helped to get his mind off breasts more than manual labor. And right now, he was going to do so much manual labor he planned on working himself into exhaustion. It was the only way to keep him from falling into yet another woman's bed…and possibly another woman's web.

Chapter 7

Theodore finally returned to Foodies after walking around the block a few times with his face burning with embarrassment. Why on earth did he think that Amazonian, Tarrintino-loving woman was Dana? And why on earth would he see Dana walking down the streets of Grand Rapids, Michigan when she belonged in his fantasy world of Las Vegas, Nevada? The chances of actually seeing her again were absolutely beyond microscopic. Dana Kupiac had as much chance of walking past him on the street as did Jesus.

Just then another woman in a red jacket walked past, and Theodore turned rapidly to study the window display of a shoe store. He would now and forever be terrified of women in red jackets. He'd dream of a hoard of giants in red jackets, pummeling him and saying, "You mutherfucker!"

Of course, now that he thought about it, it was rather funny. If Sarah had been with him while he mistook that Angelique for Dana, she'd have been mortified. Of course, if Sarah had been with him, he'd never have been able to get away from her long enough to make such an embarrassing mistake.

Once the second woman in a red jacket had passed, Theodore breathed a sigh of relief and continued walking. He stopped at the Asian restaurant XO and ordered a few lunches to go. He figured that Asian would be the perfect lunch choice. Mike was on a spiritual journey right now. What Theodore could figure out from it was that it involved heavy amounts of incense, stretching, and Asian cuisine. Ten minutes later, his arms heavy with plastic containers filled with pad thai with tofu, green curry chicken, and beef with onions, as well as rice and wontons, Theodore trudged back to Foodies.

Mike opened the door for him. A small blessing as Theodore could honestly see dropping the tower of food all over the newly cleaned floor. He'd been gone less than an hour, and already the place looked different. The shelving unit was up and the floor was mopped…and there were two colorful jars of preserves on the counter.

"You just missed quite the adventure," Mike said, grabbing the black takeout containers from Theodore and setting them on the counter. They grabbed chairs and made a makeshift table. There was just room enough to hold the various containers and plastic utensils.

"Yeah, well you missed quite the adventure outside," Theodore said. "Hey, guys, come on over. I got us lunch." He motioned to the construction workers and the three men joined them at the counter.

"What happened outside?" Mike said and passed out paper plates.

"I was attacked by a giant. Actually, I sort of attacked her first. I didn't mean to, I thought she was someone else. I thought she was…" Theodore paused and looked at the jars.

"Who?" Mike said. He could only manage the one word because he—along with all the other men—was shoveling rice noodles and spicy green sauce into his mouth.

"Just a woman I met in Vegas," Theodore said. He tried to say it casually.

"Yeah, I met a woman in Vegas once," one of the workers with a scruffy red beard said. "Now I pay child support."

Theodore shrugged. "It wasn't like that. I'm engaged."

"Being engaged doesn't stop a man from acting on primal urges," Mike said. "Heck. I've been married three times and that hasn't stopped me from my primal urges. The only thing that can stop me from my primal urges is…" Mike paused to think about it. "Politics. Politics makes me go soft as a boiled egg." The men grunted in agreement. "Anyway, Theodore. What just happened to you was cosmic. It was a sign," Mike finished.

"A sign of what?" Theodore knew something was coming. Ever since Mike split from his third wife, he'd become a little New Age, even though New Age seemed to be something people were into about twenty years ago. Theodore suspected Mike even wore a crystal around his neck, but he couldn't be sure.

"If you thought you saw this Las Vegas woman, your mind's eye *did* see her and it was telling you something. It was telling you that maybe you *ought* to see her, engaged or not, and so then you saw her and then the woman you thought was her attacked you and…" Mike stopped there and took an enormous bite of his eggroll. He practically eviscerated the little thing.

"And?" Theodore asked. He'd almost thought Mike was on to something.

"I dunno. Hey. Some lady dropped off some jam. I haven't tried it yet, but she had a lovely aura to her. Sort of orange and lemony. Citrus like. I think I'm going to ask her out."

"Date her, fine. Just please don't get married again," Theodore said. He pushed his plate aside. He'd suddenly lost his appetite. While the other men ate, he walked over to the jars and picked one up. It looked familiar. He turned the jar until he saw the label. DANA'S DELIGHTS. And then, really, he started to believe in signs. Of course, the label itself was a sign, wasn't it? Suddenly, he felt his heart begin to race. It wasn't possible. Couldn't be. Dana, his Dana, Dana of Las Vegas and laughter and a crazy fake wedding with Elvis and organ music…she couldn't be here, in Michigan of all places. Could she?

Theodore immediately opened the jar. It was Raspberry Ribbon, and it smelled sweet and summery and…comforting somehow. "Mike…did a woman with dark hair and brown eyes and a quirky little smile drop this off?" He tried to hide the intensity of his voice, but it still came through.

"Yeah, man, that was her. She's no model, really, but she has this air about her. I'm seriously going to ask her out."

"No. You can't."

"What do you mean I can't? Why not?"

And before Theodore could stop himself, he said, "Because she's my wife." It was the easiest way he could think of to get his friend and partner Mike Sparrow to back off, because women, once they saw Mike, looked right past Theodore. Something told Theodore that this time, he couldn't allow that to happen. He'd been pretty much invisible to every woman in his life, including his fiancée, but Dana was one woman he wanted to see him. Really see him. And if these two jars sitting in the middle of his new store weren't a sign of something cosmic, Theodore didn't know what was. At this point, if Jesus walked in the door and asked for some green curry, Theodore wouldn't be surprised at all. He was starting to believe.

"It's sort of a long story." He sat back down at the makeshift table with the guys and told them about his little adventure in Las Vegas and what it could possibly mean for his very real wedding next month. He told it to them plainly that he'd gone to Vegas to find food ideas and had made a…friend…as corny as that sounded. And they'd gone to seminars together, buffets, and had that sort of crazy whirlwind of time together that could only be summarized in movies by an awkward montage with rising music. "And then on the last night, we thought it would be hysterical to, you know, do what people do in Vegas."

"Get a sex change?" asked the skinny worker.

"No!" Theodore said. "Do people do that in Vegas?"

The skinny guy shrugged. "I might've heard something like that."

"No. We decided it would be funny to get married. You know. Hitched. Like in a chapel. So she dressed like Madonna, and I dressed like Billy Idol and we…"

"Had a white wedding?" asked Mike.

Theodore nodded.

After hearing the story, the worker with the scruffy red beard shook his head and ran his hand through his hair. "Dude," he said. "That is some kind of fucked up shit. First off, I don't see why you want to get married so bad that A) you're engaged and B) you have a practice marriage in Vegas. Who wants to be married anyway? I've got oats to sow. Wild oats."

"Yeah, right," Petey, the skinny construction worker, said. "Ed, you think you have wild oats, but really you've only got *one* oat. And her name is Samantha. And you've been dating for like seven years so you're as good as married."

"No, I'm not. If there's no ring and no paperwork, then you can still benefit from your woman treating you like a date instead of a doormat."

The skinny man looked at him. "You asked her and she refused, didn't you."

The man with a beard nodded. His eyes filled with tears. "Turned me down flat. Dammit it all, I love that woman. I'd marry her right now if she was here. And there was a preacher and people to throw rice and stuff."

"I've been married three times," said Mike. "And there's nothing quite as spiritual as bonding over and over and over again with a woman you call your wife." The men looked at him. "That was too much information, wasn't it?" They nodded. "Okay, but still. You've got to admit there's something weird about meeting a woman in Vegas, having this long night of unbelievable sex…"

"We didn't actually have sex," Theodore said softly.

"What?" The men seemed to say collectively. Ed shook his head. Petey looked like his heart was broken. And the third construction worker, Rodrigo, who had remained silent throughout the conversation, took the last eggroll and bit into it, sadly.

"That's even weirder," Mike continued. "You go to Vegas. You go and you're engaged to a lovely but Type A personality woman. In Vegas you meet this quirky free spirit who you don't have sex with…"

"We made out," Theodore offered, "in an elevator."

The men nodded in approval. Mike continued, "You make out with her, pretend to marry her, say your goodbyes to her, and then a week later, she drops off two jars of jam in your new store. I think this has got to mean something, doesn't it?"

Theodore looked at all the men. What could it mean?

Rodrigo surprised them all by speaking. He had just finished licking a spoon of jam from Dana's Delights. Rodrigo had a thick Spanish accent and it seemed to give his words an other-worldly weight. "I know what this means. It means you must find her. You must talk to this woman one more time. You are married spiritually, and you must either break that spiritual bond and marry your fiancée or you must break your fiancée's heart, and date, possibly marry, this other woman. And you must also get her recipe for this jam because it is so good I would make love to it. If it was a woman." He licked the spoon once more.

The men stared at the jar of jam for a moment then they finished their meal and got back to work.

Chapter 8

"Mom, so I made a list of my favorite foods. Could you write them down for me?" Zach asked Dana. They were at the dinner table eating meatloaf, edamame, and mashed potatoes. Zach, at aged almost-six, liked her to write things down and then read it to him later.

"We're eating right now. Can it wait?"

Zach shook his head vehemently, so fiercely that Dana had a momentary image of Zach's head separating from his body and then flinging across the table. She blamed motherhood for images like that. One day she was perfectly normal; after having kids, she was saying things like, "Put down that fork! You're going to puncture a lung!"

Zach stopped the head thing. "Mom. Seriously. It's actually really important. Really, really important. You need to make this list."

Dana sighed and put her paper towel on the table. "Ruby, eat some meatloaf. Zach, eat some edamame." Her kids were on opposite ends of the food spectrum currently. Ruby wanted to eat only vegetables and fruit, and Zach was becoming a fierce carnivore. Their dad and his new wife were virtually vegetarians so Dana understood. She grabbed a pen and her grocery list from the fridge, flipped it over and sat back down. "Okay, Zach. Go."

He rattled off his list as if she was timing him. "I like meatloaf, meatballs, and meat sauce, and I like meat. And I like ham. And bacon. And is cheese a meat?"

"Cheese is a cheese," Dana said.

Ruby said with a mouthful of edamame beans, "It's got milk in it."

Zach considered this. "Okay. That means it came from meat so I like cheese. And I like sandwiches, but only if there's meat in it. Annnd…" he thought deeply. "I also like ice cream because that also has milk in it and that comes from meat too. That's it."

Dana scribbled the rest of his list down and tried to suppress her smile. The idea of ice cream coming from meat was vaguely horrifying. "Okay," she said. "Done and done." She picked up her fork and took a bite of meatloaf. Eating meatloaf still made her feel like a kid. She preferred stuffed pasta or Indian food with lots of veggies and beans and possibly chicken in it, but for her kids, she'd cook their favorites.

"Mom…" Ruby said the word as if it were the beginning of a song.

"Yes."

"When you going to get married again?"

Dana almost choked on her meatloaf. She swallowed. Took a sip of her wine and then looked at her two kids who were now staring intently at her, not blinking, not eating. It was as if an eerie fog of silence had fallen over their dinner table. Dana spoke softly. "I'm not planning on getting married any time soon, so you don't have to worry, Peanut."

"I'm not *worried*," Ruby said. "Zach…Zach and me…we *want* you to get married. We talked about it, right Zach?"

"Yep."

Ruby, apparently as spokesperson for this particular conversation, continued, "Dad has a wife. You're a mom. You should have a husband."

Dana was fairly certain their dad must've been asking them questions. Questions that were probably slightly inappropriate. She could just hear him saying, "So, kiddos, your mom bringing any friends over? Does she have sleepovers? When is she going to get you a new dad? Huh? Wouldn't you like to have two dads?" Dana knew that her ex would very much like it if he didn't have to pay child support anymore, something Dana promised he wouldn't as soon as she could financially support herself and the kids. No doubt from Paul's perspective a husband would help her do this.

The trouble was, Dana wasn't looking for a husband. She'd tried that. She was a wife and a mom and then somehow she'd gone hollow. Plus, if she ever got married again, she wanted it to be with someone she loved. Someone who understood and supported her, who loved the kids and treated them kindly. And after the dating horror stories she'd heard, she thought meeting and marrying Bigfoot might be an easier feat than meeting and marrying a single forty-something-year-old available man who wanted kids and was okay if the kids weren't actually his own.

She put her fork down, her appetite evaporated. "Look, guys, there are all kinds of families. Can you tell me a few kinds? Like, there are families with a mom and a dad, and families with a dad and a stepmom, and families with just a mom like ours."

"At school, Caleb has two dads," Zach said.

"Exactly," Dana said. "A dad and a step-dad."

"Nooooo. Caleb has two *dads*. They had a wedding and everything. Caleb got to carry the ring *and* he didn't have to wear shoes. They were married on *the beach.*"

She nodded. "Yes. See? Good. Okay…so yes, there are families with two dads.."

"Or two moms!" shouted Ruby.

"Or two moms," Dana agreed. "There are families with grandparents and…" She was about to say there were some unfortunate kids out there who didn't have families at all, but she stopped herself. "Anyway. I'm your mom and I love you and right now our family is Mommy, Zach and Ruby. And Aunt Valerie and Uncle Vick and your grandma and grandpa and your dad and his wife and…"

"We know, Mom," Zach said. "We know. We just…"

"Mom, we just want you to be happy," Ruby said. "Hey, Mom, I'm eating my meatloaf. I'm eating it!" Ruby opened her mouth wide to prove that she was, indeed, eating it.

Dana nodded and smiled and tried to keep the tears she was feeling tucked safely away.

Chapter 9

After the kids were tucked in for the night, Dana did her nightly routine of picking up the effluvia that represented her life as a mom to two young kids. She put the Star Wars action figures in their green bin, separated the tiny plastic Squinkies and put them in the yellow bin. She picked up pieces of paper and crayons and pipe cleaners and seashells and, for some reason, cleaned up a pile of sand that had somehow appeared on her kitchen floor. Either Zach had attended his friend Caleb's dads' wedding, or he'd carried sand home in his shoes from a playground.

By 8:30, Dana had her feet kicked up and a second glass of wine. She thought of the endless things she could do. She could check email. That was high entertainment. Read a book, but she'd probably fall right to sleep. She could begin her workout routine that promised to shape her ass, lift her boobs, and make her ten years younger.

She did the only thing that sounded good to her. She called her sister. "Valerie," she said without preamble. "I'm ready to date."

Her sister gasped. "Shut the front door! I'll be right over."

Chapter 10

An hour later, Valerie was sitting in Dana's kitchen and Dana poured her the last of the bottle of wine. "I figure I have two hours, maybe two and a half," Valerie said. "I pumped to within an inch of my life, and Vick has enough milk in the refrigerator now to make mousse."

"Ew," Dana said.

"Breast milk mousse for the twins. Yeah. Sounds gross but you wouldn't believe the shit I read about in magazines for new moms. I totally believe that somewhere out there is a freelance writer telling me that the only way my children are going to develop a healthy brain is if I feed them breast milk and make mousse from it. Fuckers. It's like the advertising world thinks that as soon as you give birth, all of your time and energy goes to your kids."

"I'm glad you aren't buying into all that."

Valerie took a huge sip of wine. "I can't buy into it. If I listen to everything they say I'm supposed to be doing for the babies like practicing times tables and reading Dickens, I'll be in the fetal position. Like, permanently." She paused. "I'm really attracted to the *Victorian* way of childrearing. Ignore them."

They laughed.

"Are you okay, Val?" Dana asked after a moment. Valerie was the toughest woman she knew, let alone the toughest mom. She rarely complained. For her to actually be drinking wine and venting meant that she'd definitely reached a breaking point.

"I'm fine. I'm just tired, lactating, Vick wants to have sex with me, and all I want right now is a weekend of bubble baths and romance novels."

Dana nodded. "You'll have that again," she paused, "in about eighteen more years."

"By that time, my boobs will be so droopy they'll have met my knees. Hello knees!"

"Oh, they will not. And even if they did," Dana said, "Vick won't care. He'll just be happy he gets to see you naked again."

"Yep. In eighteen years." Val finished off her wine. "That was lovely. And…shit…I can feel my milk coming in. Please, please get my mind off feeling like a dairy cow. Let's talk about finding you a date."

Where should they start? Dana wondered. It wasn't as if she could decide she wanted to date and then a whole line of firm, eligible, shirtless bachelors appeared before her. She was momentarily distracted by imaging a whole line of firm, eligible, shirtless bachelors standing in front of her. One of them looked like Colin Firth, of course—though he was wearing a cute sweater—and the rest were construction workers, the young and firm kind, not the beer belly kind.

"Hello?" Valerie said. "Earth to Dana."

"Sorry," she said. "I had a mini-fantasy there. Okay," she continued, "how do I go about dating? I don't know anyone *to* date. And according to The Rules, I'm not supposed to approach the man. The man is supposed to approach me."

"The Rules? Didn't we read that, like, forever ago? Whatever. That's bull. When I met Vick, I was stinking drunk and I walked up to him and told him he needed to get in my bed immediately."

Dana laughed. It was true. "Well, it's a little different now." She didn't say all the things she was thinking, but there were a lot of thoughts going on. Somehow for a man, if he had kids and was divorced, he was more eligible. It was as if he had some kind of sheen to him that attracted young, pretty women. A single dad somehow looked like he was more together, more approachable, more…amenable. But for Dana, she felt as if because she had kids, she was instantly a woman with "issues". A single mom sort of felt like some kind of proclamation to the world, shouting that you just couldn't handle things and you were about an inch from going Mommy Dearest. Like a man who would even be the slightest bit interested in her would run scared as soon as he saw her zombie and princess standing next to her. What kind of man would possibly find her attractive as a woman, but also as a mom?

"I think I just changed my mind," Dana said. "This is too hard. I don't know anyone I could possibly date. Maybe it's just enough to say that I'm interested in dating, and the universe will provide something."

"Yep," Valerie agreed. "The universe will provide something. It's called the Internet. I know it's not pretty, Dana, but you aren't going to meet anyone by being with your kids all the time. And if you meet anyone at the college, then they're probably underage and your student. So…until there's something better…there's always online dating."

Dana nodded reluctantly. It was true. If she wanted to date, she'd probably have to go online to do it. It's not as if this were Vegas, and she could just meet and connect with someone. And, of course, Theo was really only a fantasy anyway. In Vegas, she hadn't been all of her roles like mom, and adjunct professor, and divorcee. She'd just been Dana.

And, oh, how she wanted to just be Dana again…at least for a little while with dating. "Okay, let's check it out. I don't want to do a profile or anything, I just want to take a look and see who's out there."

Valerie nodded and they moved to the computer. Dana tried not to hear scary Psycho music as she approached.

Chapter 11

Mike turned off all the lights in Foodies, punched in the code for the alarm, and locked the doors behind him. It was late out, the streetlights in downtown Grand Rapids twinkling. They really were twinkling. They had Christmas lights or something strung up in all the trees lining Monroe Center. He supposed it was to make the place look cheerful and festive. Mostly it just made him tired.

Actually, working in the store today had made him tired, which was his exact goal. He needed to be just shy of sheer exhaustion to keep himself from making any big mistakes. As he walked up the street to his Heritage Hill apartment, he thought that at least he hadn't put the moves on that Dana woman. Theodore was his best and longest friend. He'd already lost all his money, his home, and his third wife; he couldn't afford to lose his only friend. Plus, as much as he'd thought the Dana woman was attractive, he'd really only been interested in having her with him naked for a few hours. Then he'd move on.

His apartment was only a few blocks from Foodies. He could've chosen one of the downtown hotels, but that was too depressing to him. Hotels were so sterile and so soulless. He really was trying to change his life a bit, and he couldn't do that from a hotel room. Instead, he'd had the luck to stumble upon a furnished room in an old Victorian house. There was a For Rent sign and he'd immediately called the owner. Her voice had been young, and he'd heard a baby crying in the background. She'd said her mother was touring Italy, but she could rent him the room on a month-to-month basis. Once her mother got home, she'd decide if he could stay or not.

It didn't bother Mike. He wasn't planning on staying any longer than he had to. He just wanted to get Foodies up and running, recharge his life, and then return to the suburbs of Detroit to run their other store. Of course, once he returned there, he'd have to book another hotel. The thought of looking to buy something new again was too overwhelming.

He walked up the long hill on Fountain, his thighs screaming at him. He really needed to work out more. It must be that he needed more exercise and not that he was getting old. He couldn't even bear to think about that possibility.

When he reached the green house with the giant porch, he noticed immediately that something was different. His apartment was on the first floor. The owner lived on the top floor. For the last month, the top floor had been quiet and dark but now…now…he looked up. The windows were open and he could swear he could smell oranges. Freshly peeled oranges. He heard opera music floating through the air.

And then he saw the silhouette of a woman standing at the window. Looking at him. He couldn't see what she looked like but he could see enough to know that she had the figure of a 1950s starlet.

He reached for his keys to the lock in the door, suddenly feeling just a little more energized.

Maybe it was too soon to change his ways. Maybe he could have a little fun first before giving up women and relationships entirely.

Chapter 12

Theodore was staring at the computer screen.

"You're staring at the computer screen," echoed Sarah. "What are you doing anyway? You've been there forever. Look, all of the planning is nearly done and if you're researching something for your silly little store, it can wait. It is Wednesday, Theodore. And that means we're going to Do It. And I'd like to Do It now because I have two episodes of The Bachelor recorded, and I want to watch that."

He tried to respond. He really did, but inwardly Theodore felt like he was frozen. He no more wanted to Do It with Sarah than he wanted to make sweet love to the computer screen he was staring at. "Sarah, I'm not feeling all that well."

Sarah came up behind him; she stood there breathing for a bit, then reached her hand in front of him and grabbed him between his legs. "Ouch!" he said.

"Give me a second here and I'll see if I can get you feeling better. But really, Theodore, I only have like fifteen minutes for this." She began to rub him.

He pushed her hand away. "Sarah, I'm just not…I don't want…I'm not in the mood."

She squinted at him. "It's this whole 'what happened in Vegas' thing isn't it?"

Theodore took a deep breath and looked at the computer one more time. He'd been researching Dana's Delights, gourmet jams and jellies, and had found her. Dana. His Dana. The woman he'd met and known for two short days and couldn't stop thinking about. The kicker was…she lived in Coopersville, Michigan. Coopersville! The small town tucked between farms and factories was just a twenty-five minute drive from where he was now. It wasn't possible, and yet, it was true.

"Let's sit down, Sarah," he said and moved to the couch. After a moment Sarah followed him.

"I don't really want to have a heart to heart with you, Theodore."

"We need to."

"No, we don't. I don't want to know about Vegas. Whatever stupid stuff you did there, it stays there, okay? You just need to stop moping around and get over it."

"I can't get over it, Sarah. I've tried. I can't stop thinking about…"

"What's his name?" Sarah said resolutely.

Theodore wasn't sure he heard right. "Excuse me?"

"You hooked up with a dude, right. What's his name?"

He didn't know quite how to respond. That Sarah was so blasé about his possibly having an affair, and an affair with another man was absolutely shocking to him. And sort of funny. "I did not hook up with a dude."

Sarah nodded. "Then we don't have anything to talk about. There's one week until Thanksgiving and my family coming over. I don't want to hear another word about anything even remotely stressful until we get through that. I want it to be perfect and not a train wreck, and then I want to focus on the wedding. It's in six weeks, Theodore. Six."

It sounded like a death sentence. Then Theodore found the words that he'd been wanting to say for so long. If he were being honest with himself, he'd known for months that he didn't want to marry Sarah. They'd been together for two years, and had he ever really felt like she was The One? No. Mostly, he'd felt swept away by inertia. He didn't actively want to remain a bachelor for his entire life. He wanted a family, a wife, kids. He also wanted passion and humor. For a long time he'd thought he just hadn't met The One, then after dating Sarah he'd just resigned himself that what he wanted in a relationship wasn't possible. So, when Sarah proposed to him by saying, "Look, you either marry me in January or I dump you," he had gone to the store and bought the ring she'd put on hold. Now, though, after a taste of what fun was, after a series of kisses that lasted no more than a few moments, Theodore realized that he'd been wrong. Wildly, deeply wrong. You couldn't marry someone you felt obligated to. It only hurt both of you.

"I can't marry you, Sarah. And I don't want to just get through Thanksgiving. I should've insisted we visit my family. I actually like my family, as quirky and embarrassing as they are." The words started flowing and Theodore found he didn't want to stop them. "And I'm terribly sorry, but I don't want to marry you in January either. I'm sorry. I can't. We aren't right together."

Sarah bit her lip. "We're totally right together. Look how good we look in our engagement picture." She motioned to the picture on his mantle. Just moments before the photo, she'd told him to suck in his gut and smile and try not to look so stupid. She'd gotten the picture she'd wanted. They were smiling and looked attractive and well-adjusted, but it was all an illusion.

"You don't get married based on how you look together," he said the words quietly, gently. Sarah said nothing for a while, and then he felt her begin to tremble. It wasn't sadness, though, but rage.

"You asshole!" she screamed and then jumped to her feet. "I am thirty years old. All of my friends are married. You're successful. You have a nice house. I'll have sex with you, and we can have a kid or whatever, and we are getting married. I don't care what you say…we…are. And don't mention Vegas. I honestly don't care who you slept with or kissed or whatever. I've had my share of flings too, Theodore. It's biological. It doesn't mean anything. What means something is that picture on the mantel. So stop being stupid. Just get upstairs, and we'll have make up sex, and I'll even delay my program for a while. We'll just pretend none of this ever happened."

Theodore did so want to pretend that none of this had ever happened. Unfortunately, what he wanted to pretend that had never happened wasn't his experience in Vegas, he wanted to pretend his *relationship* had never happened. "I can't marry you," he said again, only this time with a firm certainty. Inertia was taking over again, and this time it was the inertia of honesty. "Sarah…I can't marry you because…" then he knew he could only tell her the truth, "when I was in Vegas, I married someone else. And her name is Dana Kupiac." He stood up. "I'm sorry."

Sarah just looked at him. Silence hung heavy in the air. And then she smacked him across the face. Hard. The sound of the smack resonated in the air for a moment. Neither one of them moved. "Take it back," she said through gritted teeth.

"I can't take it back. It happened," he said softly. "I'm sorry."

"Take the wedding back. Get it annulled or whatever. You were drunk and stupid and high or whatever. Did you even fill out the paperwork?"

Theodore tried to focus on what she was saying. Didn't she hear him? He'd just confessed to not only an affair, but an actual marriage. "We didn't…I don't know… We thought it would be funny so we got dressed up and we went to a chapel…"

"But you didn't get a marriage license first?" Sarah stared at him intently. "You just went to the chapel, right? You just pretended to get married. You didn't actually get married."

It occurred to him that what she was saying was probably true. Hadn't he said his vows, though? Did "Oy!" count as a vow? He could barely find his words. He'd been so close to standing up to Sarah for once, for saying how he really felt, and now it seemed as if it was all slipping away from him.

Sarah kissed his cheek. She was sugary sweet again, as if everything that had just happened had been nothing but a brisk wind and had now passed. "Look, Theodore, we all do stupid things," she said, her voice like happy bells. "I mean, you are not the kind of person that does something spontaneously. That's what I love about you. And it's sort of cute that you couldn't even get a wedding right. You have to get a marriage license first. You were stressed out. This wedding is a lot of work. I know! I'm so stressed out right now I could eat an entire slice of cake. But we've got to stay in control. You and me. Okay? In control. I forgive you. I forgive everything you did in Vegas. Just don't talk about it again." With the next line, her voice was like barbed wire again. "I mean it, Theodore. I don't want to talk about it again. Ever."

He said nothing. What was there to say? Sarah was right. He did one spontaneous thing in his entire life, and he couldn't even get that right.

Sarah reached for her jacket. "Look, my fifteen minutes are gone now. We can Do It tomorrow, I guess. I've got a meeting with Mother and the caterer. We're going to discuss the drinks. They wanted to do some crazy foreign sounding drink, but I just want it classy. Beer, wine, champagne. That's the kind of people we are. Love you." She kissed his cheek again. In moments, she was gone.

Theodore stared at the computer screen. Dana's Delights stared back at him. If he closed his eyes, he could still feel the warmth of her near him. He wasn't even imagining kissing her anymore, just standing next to her. Hearing her laugh.

Before he could stop himself from thinking too deeply, Theodore did one more spontaneous thing. He sent Dana's Delights an email.

Chapter 13

Before Mike was even able to open the door he heard the latches unfasten and the door swung open; the scent of orange blossoms and summer rain spilled out over him.

"You must be Mr. Sparrow," a low and luscious voice said.

He blinked a few times, trying to see the woman who stood in the doorway to his apartment. You entered the foyer and then turned left for his apartment or went up the stairs for…hers. "I'm Mavis Williams. I'm your landlord." She held out her hand. He took it in his and felt an immediate surge sweep through him. The woman practically popped with sexual energy.

"Don't you mean land*lady*?" he asked coyly. Sure, he'd sworn off getting trapped into a woman's web, but that was before meeting a woman as curvy and sexually energized as this one. Mike had an immediate vision of creeping up the stairs at night, having his way with this woman, and then walking downstairs to the comfort of his own bedroom. It would be a perfect set up. In fact, he might not even need to talk to her at all.

He tried to get a better look at her face, but it was dark out, and the light in the hallway wasn't on. All he could see was the outline of her sensual body, smell the delicious scent of oranges, and he could see plenty of her curves. She was wearing some kind of silky robe, and it flowed over her the way he imagined water would.

"I prefer land*lord*. I rather like being in charge. Come in. I hear from my daughter that you want to stay on a month-to-month lease."

Mike was confused. Her daughter? He'd totally forgotten that he'd rented from her daughter who'd had a crying infant in the background. And if this woman's daughter had an infant, then that meant that this woman was…a grandmother.

Mavis stepped into the foyer, letting him in and turned on the hallway light. It took a moment for his eyes to adjust and then he just stared at her. Mavis's hair was entirely silver and sparkled in the hallway light.

"I…Yes… My…" he stammered.

Mavis seemed to study him for a moment. He felt her eyes move over his chest, down his waist, and take in every inch of him. He'd done the same thing to women, but it had never been done to him. She seemed to make a decision. "Something's happening here, Mr. Sparrow. You should know that I'm fifty-eight years old, I have two children and five grandchildren. I am not at all interested in a relationship. I will not give you my heart, nor do I want any part of yours. But I will take this from you…"

She leaned forward and kissed him.

And Mike was utterly…transported.

Chapter 14

At five in the morning, Dana was wrapped in her pink robe and seated at her computer. If she was lucky, she'd have an hour or so of uninterrupted quiet before the kids woke up. This was her time to work for herself. She had the day to focus on her students and then the afternoon and evening for her kids, but these precious few minutes in the morning generally was all she managed to eke out for herself. By 8:30 at night, when the kids were finally tucked into bed, she was too tired for anything, except maybe chocolate mousse with orange liquor.

She wasn't checking online dating ads. The list of available men had been depressing, to say the least, last night.

"Look at this one!" Valerie had offered, trying to stay upbeat. "He has hair!"

"That's a toupee. And a bad one," Dana had said.

"Well, everyone needs love," Valerie had said.

They'd looked at a couple of sites and there were, Dana admitted, decent looking men. It just felt wrong to her somehow. Didn't dating online do the exact thing she hated? It reduced a potential relationship to whether you were attracted to a person or not. If you weren't, click. Next. It left little room for the mystery of chemistry, that strange thing that happened when you met someone and felt something electrical, something stirring between you. Chemistry could make someone plain look beautiful to you. Like what had happened when she met Theodore.

Enough of thinking about that.

Dana and her sister had agreed that maybe they'd shelve the online dating idea for a little bit. They could always return to it. Valerie had left Dana, instead, with strict instructions to start feeling like she was available, so that she'd send out those strange pheromone signals. Dana had promised.

She sniffed herself. She didn't notice any pheromone signals. Mostly, she just thought she needed a shower.

Plenty of time for that later. Right now, she wanted to savor the quiet and check her email. With Thanksgiving just one week away, Dana thought/hoped/prayed that there would be a few orders on her website. She already had enough pickles and jams and preserves to stock a small store, all of them waiting in her basement, stacked neatly on shelves. She thought she'd also offer a special holiday preserve. Something for lovers maybe. Something with chocolate and orange liquor—for some reason she kept thinking of that combination. Must have been something in the air.

She opened her email. To her delight she did indeed have three messages from her website. One was from one of her coworkers at the community college ordering two jars of bread and butter pickles…and one was an order to ship a holiday assortment to New York City. New York City! Some of her online ads were actually starting to pay off.

Then Dana wondered if people in New York actually ate something as mundane as toast with jam? Dana imagined that the women there pranced around in stilettos and clothing so chic you automatically developed a French accent when you put it on. Of course, maybe they'd put her jam on goat cheese and fig leaves or something. But the pickles. The order requested pickles too. And did men in New York like little pickles like hers? For some reason, yeah, she could see men in New York liking pickles.

Then she opened the third email with the re: section listed as Emergency Thanksgiving Order. Dana's heart stopped. She started drooling. She fell to the floor in a fit and started barking.

No. She didn't actually do any of those things. She just opened the email.

It wasn't possible. No. No! It wasn't possible! She'd only had her business up and running for a few weeks. She'd only just returned from Vegas. With her order from Jennie and the two online and the two cases for Foodies, she had just enough to keep her busy, and make a nice little profit. But this…

She read the email again and checked the attached order form with the PayPal information. The owner of a gourmet store—another one!—was looking to order a selection of preserves from her. It was an emergency order, and the customer was hoping to pick up five cases from her before the holiday. Dana looked at the calendar. Thanksgiving was next week and the customer wanted the preserves and side orders this weekend.

Dana whispered a string of obscenities and then double-checked her PayPal. The money was all there. This person had actually ordered a small fortune of her product, but it was too much. She wasn't prepared for this. How could she do this? How could she handle it?

"Mom!" she heard Ruby's voice call to her. "I want apple juice!"

Dana took a deep breath and smiled to herself. Of course she could handle it. She could handle it because she was a single mom, and she had no other choice but to handle it. She also liked the challenge of filling all these orders. Most of the orders could be filled from what she already had on stock. The rest, she'd work on this weekend. She typed a quick response to the man, a Mr. Lucky Jackson, and gave him the address to her friend's restaurant. She prepared the preserves during the restaurant's off hours and gave Stella a small percentage of profits. Truth be told, she paid that percentage in free jams for the restaurant, but it was a good arrangement. One day Dana would have a professional kitchen, but until then, she'd fake it. She'd have the gentleman pick up the order at the restaurant, saving time and money in shipping, and that way he wouldn't know where she lived. After seeing the online dating site…well…she just wanted to be careful.

She really could handle this, she knew. She could more than handle this. She could excel at this. After everything she'd been through in the last year, hadn't she already excelled? She realized she sort of lived her entire life that way right now…and damned if that didn't feel good.

"Ruby, you can get up now!" she called out as she closed her laptop. "I'll get your juice!" It was the start of a new day, but this one had just a little more promise in it.

Chapter 15

"You did *what*?" Mike asked incredulously.

"I ordered more preserves from her. We can stock some in the Detroit store…and I'm going to make up baskets for the holidays, featuring local business goods." Theodore said calmly. True, his initial order as Lucky Jackson (the character Elvis played in "Viva Las Vegas") had been impulsive, but after he'd acted on the plan, he sat down and justified it. They really could use her product, and it was a superior one. And it was local.

"I'm not talking about the *effing* preserves, Theodore. I mean…you broke up with Sarah? You dumped her?" Mike really sounded like he couldn't believe it. In fact, he was so nonplussed that he'd stopped unpacking the wine from boxes and stood there holding a bottle of Chataneuf du Pape in his hand. He looked as if at any moment it would slip from his hand and crash to the floor…or he might break the bottle open and use it as a weapon. Both images were disturbing.

"Yeah. I did. For a minute I did and then…she slapped me and then she forgave me and…"

"And you got back together," Mike said. Theodore thought he sounded a little bit sad about that.

"I'm committed to her," Theodore said.

"Committed is right. You do realize that's the same word they use for putting someone in an institution. And there's a reason they call marriage an institution."

Theodore gently took the bottle of his favorite vintage from his partner's hands and gingerly placed it on the shelf with the others. Mike seemed really out of sorts today. He was edgy, nervous, and more than a little off-center. Bad timing for one of his moods. The store was almost ready for its opening. In just a few days, they'd have appetizers and balloons and a small press opening.

Who was he kidding? Theodore was in a mood too. He was anxious about the opening and success of Foodies, and in just one day, he was going to re-meet Dana, face to face, and Vegas far away. Theodore thought that maybe he shouldn't be so excited to see her again. He wasn't thinking clearly. And surely it wasn't a good idea to see her. Why was he even doing this to himself? Was it some sort of test?

"So breaking up with Sarah was just a last minute cold feet thing?" Mike said, bringing Theodore back to reality.

"Yeah. Temporary," he agreed, although he sounded like he was trying to convince himself. "A temporary freak out. She's right. We're perfect for each other. I've known her for years. We've dated forever. We've got our whole life together mapped out."

Mike said nothing for a moment and then, "Well, that sounds exciting doesn't it? Having your whole life mapped out."

Theodore felt his face get hot. "So, what? You're saying just because you don't believe in the institution of marriage that I shouldn't get married? What's your problem, man? I know you're on divorce number three, but don't put your shit off on me."

Mike, surprisingly, nodded. "I hear you, Theodore. I hear you. I'm sorry. Normally, I'd say you're right, as I generally do like to put my shit on other people. It's a pastime of mine. But this time, I swear to you, I'm just trying to ask you a couple of questions to get you thinking. Questions like, you know, if you're so happy with Sarah, then why are you so excited about tasting Dana's Delights again? Because you did…right…taste them? In Vegas, right?"

"I'm ignoring you," Theodore said. "And where's all your Zen Buddha now? I'm not trying to taste her delights. I just want to see her one more time. Talk to her. I mean, aren't you supposed to say I did the right thing, that there are no coincidences in life, only opportunities missed and opportunities taken? Doesn't it mean something cosmically significant that the woman I met in Vegas, the woman I made out with and eventually 'married'…in Vegas…doesn't it mean something that she actually stopped over here? And left jam? Aren't I supposed to see her one more time? It's probably the one thing that will convince me that I'm right about Sarah. That she's the one for me." Now Theodore was the one holding a bottle of wine as if he might hurt someone with it.

Mike held up his hands in a "hey, don't hit me with that" sort of pose. "I hate to tell you this, bud, but I sort of don't buy all that new age, power of attraction stuff anymore. I think that was just a phase I was going through while I settled into single life again. No. I don't really buy any of that. Sometimes, you think you have everything planned out and then something happens and whammo! Your whole attitude changes." There was a slight pause, as if Mike was remembering something. The thought seemed to pass. "Anyway, I do think it's cool that you're taking life by the horns and…" Mike stared off into space. "I have no idea what that expression means," he finished.

"It means for once in my life I'm doing something I want to. And tomorrow, I want to drive to Coopersville and knock on my wife's door. I mean Dana's door. I'm going to knock on her door."

"And then what?"

Theodore blinked. He looked at Mike. "What do you mean and then what?"

"Then what happens? You knock on the door and then what? Do you kiss her? Thank her for the jam? Flash her? What?"

Theodore's normally erect body drooped. He had been so wrapped up in finding out a way to meet her again, face to face, without the comfort or security of emails or planned dates or phony conversations…but he hadn't once stopped to think what he would possibly say to her when he did see her. She'd think he was a stalker. She'd think he was creepy. What was he supposed to say? Did he say, "Hey, I was engaged to someone in Vegas when we, you know, and I'm still engaged though I have doubts, and hey, I just wanted to see you one more time." Did he say those things? What if he lost control and said other things, things he wasn't supposed to say or think or even feel? What if he said, "Would you want to sleep with me? Or possibly spend your entire life with me?"

"Holy shit," Theodore breathed. "I haven't a clue what happens after that. What am I doing, Mike? Why did I order those jams?"

Mike laughed. "I've got some new age books and a video called the *Secret*. It, like, tells you that you attract the things you need in life. So maybe you need some drama. A last minute shake up. You can read up on it if you want. I'm done with the whole Ask the Universe for Something and it Provides. After three wives, I think I've asked enough. Mostly, I just want to be left alone right now. Yeah. Being alone is exactly what I want." Again, Mike sounded like he was trying to convince himself of something. "But you can borrow the crap if you want to. Maybe it will work for you. I mean, you have, what, twenty-four hours to figure it out?"

Theodore glanced at his watch. Twenty-four hours. That hardly seemed like enough time to learn about everything he had to learn. Somehow, he was already feeling guilty. He felt guilty about his trip to Las Vegas and asking to see Dana again, all while he was engaged. And then he felt guilty because he knew without question that he had to see Dana again, just one more time. Maybe that was The Secret in his life. He had twenty-four hours to figure out the rest of his life. He could do that, couldn't he?

Chapter 16

With twenty-four hours before her first official customer picked up her product, Dana did the only thing she could. She called in the troops. She was going to need all the help she could get and that would mean coercing her parents, her sister and brother-in-law, her own children, and her coworker Jennie to help her out. If Dana could, she'd even put her twin baby nephews to work too. Couldn't they stir a pot or something? Or maybe with all the suckling they did, she could teach them to blow on a whistle to keep everybody motivated.

Luckily, everyone agreed and Dana breathed a little easier. For about two seconds. Then it occurred to her that she didn't actually know what she was going to prepare for the order. After teaching and picking up the kids from daycare, and then cooking them a quick dinner, and then reading stories, playing with action figures, making a snack and then dessert, giving baths, blowing noses, Dana was ready for a vacation on a desert island with a bottle of wine and a gigolo. She had to settle for surrounding herself with an assortment of cookbooks, magazines, and notes instead.

The problem with filling an order of this size and such a short deadline is that the jars would still be warm, and they wouldn't have time to ferment. That meant no pickles, green tomato chow or most chutneys. And because most of the summer fruit was now a distant memory, that also ruled out most jams and jellies. *Why? Why did I open a canning company? Why couldn't I have made chocolates or cupcakes or something easier?* she asked herself. Of course the reason for that was, she was crummy at baking and chocolate never made it far enough in the cooking process to become anything she could sell. She generally would eat all of it before she could part with it.

For a little inspiration, Dana put some classic jazz singers on her iTunes playlist. Dinah Washington, Frank Sinatra, Ella Fitzgerald…for her, these singers made her relaxed and inspired at the same time.

She took out some crackers and brie cheese, a little peach chutney, a glass of wine, and sat down in the middle of the floor prepared for inspiration to come.

What could she make that wouldn't need to be pickled and would use ingredients that were available now? Literally. Now.

She flipped through her cookbook. It was covered in notes. Her cookbooks had become a journal of sorts with dates recorded for when she first made a recipe and what she thought of it. Also, who was there with her as she ate the meal. It saddened her to see how many recipes she had cooked for Paul and how many times she had written, "Paul doesn't seem to care for it, but I love it." Wasn't that just the heart of their relationship right there? That they had divergent likes and dislikes. They'd married because they were opposites and in the end got divorced for the same reason.

Still, flipping through her notes, though making her sad, now also made her remember that there had been good times. There were summers on the back porch when she made fresh bruschetta using the tomatoes straight from their garden. The first time she'd tried green tomato chow using the tomatoes that hadn't ripened. The chow was made with green tomatoes, onions, sugar, vinegar and spices and was sweet and sour at the same time and absolutely terrific on a meat pie with a flaky crust. And there were notes for the first time she'd made an apple strudel with hints of almond and fresh raspberries. That was a warm fall day and the kids had made mud pies while she cooked. They'd eaten outside and then she'd used the hose to spray the kids clean. Paul wasn't there for that one though. At the time, he'd been on a business trip somewhere, falling in love with another woman, and falling out of love with Dana.

It still hurt, but the ache had become more like a bruise. It only hurt when pressed upon.

She turned the page of her cookbook, drawing her fingers across the entry that read, "I made this for Zach, age 11 months. He is not a fan." And then the one followed by, "Zach loves this and Ruby refuses to eat anything else." This was the recipe that she had tweaked for the kids. Perhaps this was one of the reasons Dana loved food and cooking so much.

A good meal could freeze a moment in time for you. Dana remembered, instantly, the kind of memory that was more like reliving, her children as babies and toddlers, and she knew that this was the recipe they would make tomorrow. It included Michigan cherries and pears and was sweet with a hint of tartness. In that way, it was sort of like her life.

Chapter 17

"I'm not doing it, Theodore," Sarah said, arms crossed over her chest in the way a very stubborn child would. "I am not putting that food in my mouth. It's a plant."

"It's a vegetable."

"It looks like a tree. Like a miniature bush and there are sharp spines on it."

Theodore rubbed his hand across his brow, trying to rub out the worry. "It's an artichoke, Sarah."

"And you want to serve something that has the word 'choke' in it at our wedding reception? Are you crazy? Why can't you just let me be in control of the menu? It's *my* wedding."

He pursed his lips and nodded and then pushed the plate aside. "I thought it was *our* wedding," he said quietly.

"Of course, we are getting married, but I'm the one doing the planning. You're not even supposed to want to, Theodore. Why can't you just be like every guy out there and not care about it? I want chicken and broccoli in a cheese sauce, or maybe asparagus. I love asparagus. There's nothing pokey or chokey about asparagus. Except, it does make your pee smell bad."

There were so many things he wanted to point out to her. He wanted to tell her that asparagus had the word *ass* in it, and looked like little spikes, or maybe even little skinny penises. Actually, asparagus looks like little skinny *alien* penises. He wanted to say that he was the owner of a gourmet food store so, naturally, he'd be invested in the menu. He wanted to say that not all men were as two-dimensional as his fiancée insisted they were. Instead, he did what he always did; he nodded and shut off the part of himself that cared.

"Whatever you want," he said at last.

"That's better," Sarah said. "I'm going to call Shelby now and confirm our order. And then my parents. They'll be so pleased that you're finally coming around." She patted his shoulder and then quickly ran off with her cell phone. He could hear her chattering away.

Theodore looked at his watch. Tomorrow afternoon he'd pick up the order he'd placed with Dana's Delights, the woman from Las Vegas. He could barely believe it. He was going to see her again. He yearned to see her again. There were two reasons for this. One, he wanted to know if the spark he felt for her had been because of the magic and illusion of Las Vegas…and two…if he did feel that for her, then maybe it could help him figure out what he felt for Sarah.

He'd been so certain when they'd decided to get married. It's what you did at a certain point, wasn't it? You dated, you fell in love, you got comfortable, you got married. He had been okay with his life before going to Las Vegas. He'd been fine with Sarah and their relationship. Of course, he knew that they were different, but he'd resigned himself to making it work. And now? Now?

He grabbed the plate and pulled it closer to him. The artichoke sat in front of him almost like a symbol of something, some kind of action he would take if he were only brave enough. He tore off a leaf, dipped it in the lemon butter sauce and pulled his teeth against the flesh, tasting a delicious bitter bite balanced with creamy butter.

There was a time when Theodore had known exactly where his life was going, and now he couldn't tell you what would happen in the next twenty-four hours. Somehow, he was excited about that. More excited than he probably had the right to be.

As Sarah talked rapidly about all the plans for their wedding, Theodore slowly, methodically ate the entire artichoke, down to its tender, luscious heart. Perhaps by consuming the heart of this vegetable, he could somehow figure out the emotions of his own.

Chapter 18

Mike Sparrow woke up to an empty bed, if you could call a lingering scent of orange blossoms empty. He *did* call it empty. Mavis was nowhere to be found. He knew that she wasn't in his apartment, even though he hadn't heard her leave. He could feel her absence. Strange.

He got out of bed, stretched, used the bathroom, all the while replaying what had happened last night. She'd seduced him. More than that, actually. She'd devoured him. And then she'd left. Usually Mike was the one who did the leaving, or the getting-kicked-out-of-his-own-house once his wife—times three—discovered his infidelities. With women, he used to make excuses. "I have an important meeting" or "my car is nearly out of gas and I better get to a gas station before it closes" or "I've just had a text and there's been an accident". Horrible, terrible, totally transparent lies that allowed him to escape. This morning, he didn't need to escape. Mavis had escaped first.

He turned the shower on. Crazy. It was crazy! She was twenty years older than he was, had hair as silver as a Christmas bell, had five grandchildren, two grown children and now while he lathered himself up, he couldn't seem to get his erection to go down. What was wrong with him?

He was just in a place of unrest, he told himself. His spirit needed to stretch or something. That was it. This was the universe telling him that he was doomed to repeat behavior. That's why the universe had thrust Mavis at him. Tall, delicious, exotic Mavis.

"I pledge allegiance to the flag…" he began, saying it out loud in the shower. He continued through the pledge, growing in volume until he was nearly shouting it, but it did no good. He was still hard as a rock, or, uhm, a flagpole.

He wanted her back in his bed, or on the kitchen counter, or right here in his shower and he wanted her now.

He turned the shower off, staggered out of the bathroom wrapped only in a towel, and did the only thing he could think of. He snuck up the stairs and put his still wet ear to her door. Maybe she hadn't crept out of bed because she'd had enough of him or he was a bad lover. Maybe she'd had somewhere she needed to be. Maybe there was an emergency. There had to be a reasonable explanation for this!

He could hear…laughter. Mavis was talking to someone, and she was laughing.

Mike felt his heart twist.

Ah. So this was what it felt like, he thought, to feel humiliation. Mavis had used him last night, and she'd crept away because she was done with him.

He could only hope she'd deign to use him again. It occurred to him that he was entirely at her mercy—and his erection was going nowhere.

Chapter 19

Dana was as ready as she could be. Last night, she'd called the neighborhood sitter—Kallie, age seventeen—to watch the kids while they slept and she ran to the grocery store to stock up. She bought so many supplies the checkout woman had actually said, "Is there a blizzard or something coming that I didn't hear about? Do I need to get, like, bottled water and beans or something?"

Now, a mere twelve hours later, Dana's troops were lined up in Stella's Family Diner, a tiny restaurant on Main Street in Coopersville. Coopersville was a small town, with train tracks cutting through the center of it, and a tourist train that took an exciting half hour trip to Marne and back and offered murder mysteries and pumpkins and Santa Claus visits—depending on the season of course. Dana sometimes helped out in the diner, waitressing when needed. It was a small family place and was open from 4AM until 1PM every day. After closing time, Dana could use the kitchen, thus enabling her to sell her goods without getting health officials involved. Stella had handed her the keys and the code for the alarm system. "It's all yours," she said. "Just leave me some jars by the cash register."

The restaurant was now deserted, save for the lingering smell of pancakes and coffee, and Dana's "troops". The lunch crew had just cleaned up, and Dana stood in front of her friends and family, mapping out a battle plan. Vick and Valerie were first. Each had a baby attached to them via a Bjorn. Dana felt like George C. Scott in that war movie her dad was always watching.

"Okay, Vick and Val, your job is to wrap and pack the jars. Not the ones we're cooking today, just all the other orders. You're not allowed to come into the kitchen unless you take off a baby. There will be hot juice flying."

"Ewww," Vick said.

"Stop it."

"Aye aye, Captain!" Valerie said and gave a perfect salute. "And I further promise to breast feed in the bathroom in order to protect the babies from the possibility that the soon-to-be boiling fruit might spit at them."

"A wise plan," Dana said. "Plus you don't want to burn a nipple," she whispered.

Next in line were Jennie and her boyfriend Brent. They were hipsters and both wore matching crocheted hats, long sleeved flannel shirts, and jeans with Converse, closed-toed shoes. Perfect for peeling and slicing all the fruit. "You two are in the kitchen. You're peeling and slicing. It's going to be messy and your hands might get a little red from the cherries."

"Epic," Brent said. "War wounds."

Dana calculated that the online orders would deplete her stock. She'd make enough of her special Cherry Peach Confetti to fill this new order, but they were also going to make enough jam, chutney, and dessert sauce to get through February.

Next in line came her dad and mom. Her dad had been in the Michigan National Guard until retiring six years ago at aged 65. He was taking this Jam Battle Plan seriously and had come dressed in fatigues. "Dad, you're in charge of boiling the fruit once all the ingredients are mixed. It will require precision timing."

"I'll set my watch now," he said seriously and began punching buttons on his watch.

"And Mom," Dana said, trying not to laugh. Her mom, holding a mop and a box of tissue, with her hair swept up in a handkerchief, and her shirtsleeves rolled, looked a little like Rosie from those 1940s posters. "You're on K.P. That's Kitchen Pickup. You're assigned to help clean up scraps, spills, and possibly wipe noses. Probably children's noses, but quite possibly Dad's too."

"I've been on K.P. for the last forty odd years," her mother said and Dana nodded.

And then, last in line were Dana's two kids: Ruby and Zach. Ruby was dressed in a green Hulk T-shirt and a red tutu and tights and held her favorite stuffed elephant—Elnono—close to her, and Zach was wearing his Clone Wars Halloween outfit, mask pulled down and laser gun ready.

Dana bent down to talk to them. "Kiddos, your duties are to play and have fun and never, ever go into the kitchen unless someone holds your hand—an adult holds your hand. You can't hold each other's hand." Dana was sure that under his mask, her son was rolling his eyes at her. "Okay. Everyone know what they're doing?" Dana asked.

"Yes, sir!" Her father shouted and then saluted.

"Dad, come on, I'm not a sergeant. This is going to be fun. And I really do appreciate all of you coming. Zach, get your finger out of your nose. Okay then," Dana said with a little smile. "Let's get started. Vick and Valerie, here are the order sheets, the jams, and the packing supplies. You can help with that. Jennie and Brent, come with me into the kitchen and I'll get you started on peeling and dicing. Dad and Mom…do you want to help with that or wait until we're cooking?"

Dana's mom was already unlatching a baby from Vick's chest. "I'm on Nana Patrol first," she said.

Dana's Dad said, "I once peeled two hundred and forty pounds of potatoes. By myself. With a toothpick. I think I can handle some fruit." He smiled and then walked into the kitchen.

Dana walked over to the stereo and pressed play. Rock music filled the tiny restaurant. It almost felt like a party to her. And for the first time in a very long time, Dana felt as if she didn't have to do everything entirely alone. It was enough to fill her eyes with tears, but this time, they were happy ones.

Chapter 20

There were moments in life when one's body simply moved without any thought, and this was one of those moments. After sending Sarah home last night, Theodore had flipped through cooking magazines, climbed into bed and fallen asleep. In the morning, he made crepes and bacon and drove to Foodies to keep himself occupied.

Mike was already there and they looked at each other for a moment. "You trying to get your mind off something too?" Mike asked.

Theodore nodded. He noticed that Mike looked a little rumpled and stressed out. The opening of Foodies must be getting to him too. Theodore was okay with the store opening; for him, his anxiety was all about Dana.

Yesterday, Theodore had spent most of the day trying to figure out how exactly he should talk to her. At some point, he was going to talk to her, but how was he supposed to accomplish that and not seem creepy?

He agonized over whether he should contact her before picking up the shipment he'd ordered from her. But what could he say? "Hey, I'm coming to pick up a huge order from you that I want and will use, but mostly, I just want to see you again because I can't stop thinking about you, even though I'm engaged."

The truth was, he was absolutely terrified. What if…what if she screamed when she saw him? Or attacked him with an umbrella? Women did that in movies. This was a bad idea. He knew it was a bad idea, and yet he couldn't stop himself. He'd met the woman in Vegas, and they'd agreed that what happened there stayed there, just like the commercials said.

They really did agree to it. It was jokingly at first, but there seemed to be a weight of truth to it. Maybe they both had reasons to keep their experience in Vegas actually *in* Vegas. Perhaps, now that he thought about, maybe Dana had some kind of secret life too. Maybe she was already married, and just didn't list it on her website. He thought back to the conversation, trying to discern whether or not there was something she wanted to hide.

They were at Excalibur, and Dana had turned to him, gigantic turkey drumstick in hand and said, "I love the freedom of this place. We can do anything we want and there are no repercussions." She'd taken a gigantic bite from the drumstick and then said with her mouth full, "And whatever happens here is just between us and Vegas." Then she'd looked at him meaningfully. Or maybe she was focused on chewing. Theodore wasn't sure. *Something* had happened.

At the time, he felt like it was permission to live outside himself and his life for a little while. Now, he wondered if the whole Vegas thing was actually the time he had lived *inside* his self…he'd lived authentically…for the first time in years. He wondered what Dana thought about it.

Funny, that. One would think he'd be able to just pick up the phone and call her and say, not "We'll always have Vegas", but "You know, Vegas is just a state of mind," or something equally cheesy like that. He should at least call her and admit that he was the client that was going to pick up an order from her. He reached for the phone, turned back, and then headed to the office, fully aware that Mike was following him. Theodore sat down at the computer, and then absolutely froze.

He was frozen. Well, not exactly frozen. You didn't say someone who was hyperventilating was frozen. No. You said they needed anti-anxiety medication.

"Uh-oh. Breathe, buddy," Mike said to him and handed him a paper bag to help control yet another panic attack. "I think the universe may be possibly trying to tell you something. This is about you going to see that woman, isn't it? Dana."

Theodore looked at him, wide-eyed, paper bag to lips. "You…told me you…didn't…believe in the universe and…stuff," he said between gasps.

Mike made an expression that said that was all water under the bridge. "Don't listen to me," he said. "I'm on an emotional roller coaster. I don't know what I believe from moment to moment. Just this morning I spent two hours actually waiting for a woman to knock on my door."

Theodore looked at him.

"Not just a general woman, a specific woman. Anyway. Never mind that. We need to focus on you. You're still not breathing. Take a slow, deep breath or you're going to die."

Theodore felt his heart clench, and he made a little choking sound.

Mike continued, "I meant that metaphorically. Deep breath. There you go. You think *you're* emotionally stunted and confused because you don't know if you actually want to marry your fiancée? Try ending a third marriage and having a one-night-stand with your fifty-eight-year-old lady landlord, who happens to be hotter than Sophia Loren, and she's a grandmother." Mike paused. "Didn't mean to say that last part out loud. So. Awkward transition…here's the thing, every time you try to email or call her about coming to pick up the order today, you freeze, right?"

Theodore took another deep breath in the bag and nodded.

"So don't email or call," Mike offered.

Theodore pulled the bag away from his mouth and stared at his friend. His breath seemed to return in a whoosh, though he was still confused. "What do I do then?" he asked. "Just jump up at her from behind some bushes? Yell 'oooga wooooga' or something?"

Mike seemed to consider that. "You could try knocking on her door. How about that?"

It seemed to Theodore such a magical solution, and one that was utterly foreign. With all the different types of technology there were in which one could contact someone, knocking on their door had never, ever occurred to him. "Just knock on her door?"

Mike nodded. "Look, for whatever reason, you need to see this lady. You need to. You can control that. You can't control her reaction, so there's no sense panicking. You'll know within ten seconds whether it was a smart move or not. If it is, she'll invite you in. If it's not, you'll probably see cop lights in under two minutes. Coopersville is pretty small."

One would think that this might cause Theodore to reconsider his plan. One would think he would decide to cancel the pick up, call his fiancée, and put a rest to this pointless fantasy. One would be absolutely wrong.

This was the moment when Theodore's body took over the thinking part of his brain. There were other creatures in the universe this happened to—creatures who operate solely on one need, and one need only. They were called zombies. Or possibly politicians. Theodore became one of the walking dead in that moment. How else could you explain his instant realization that, yes, he would drive to Coopersville and knock on her door. He had to pick up the cases anyway. So, yes! He would drive to Coopersville and knock on her door, and whatever happened next was beyond his control. The only thing he could control was that moment of knocking on her door. And he'd do so wearing a white sequined jumpsuit and an Elvis wig he'd purchased in Vegas as a reminder of the fun he'd had, then he'd promptly tucked it deep into the recesses of his closet.

It was appropriate to say that Theodore Drimmel was coming out of the closet, or rather, Lucky Jackson was, because in his tight jumpsuit and wig and the big dark glasses, he would look entirely like a nerd who could kick some ass. At least while karaoke-ing .

"You're going to kick ass," Mike said, as if reading his mind.

Theodore smiled. For the first time in his life, he felt like it was entirely possible.

Chapter 21

Mike did everything he could to take his mind off of Mavis. He worked out. He cleaned Foodies from top to bottom. Twice. He reorganized stock. Finally, he walked up the hill to his apartment and for a pathetic moment, stood looking up at her window longingly. All he needed was a trench coat, a boom box, and Peter Gabriel singing from its speakers to complete the picture.

He had to snap out of this. There was something seriously wrong with him. He was just out of a third marriage and was emotionally unstable and unsuitable for love.

That thought almost gave him a heart attack. Who said anything about love? Why was he thinking about love? He wasn't thinking about love. He was thinking about fucking. Just plain old, wonderful, titillating fucking.

He remembered kissing Mavis and how sweet she was. How she laughed at him when he'd tried to be all tough and sultry.

"Mike, relax. Take it slow. We have all night," she'd told him. And he had relaxed. He stopped using lines. He stopped focusing on what he wanted and needed, and had turned his attention to her. What was happening in his brain?

He actually sensed her at the window before he heard it slide open.

"You look pathetic out there, you know that?" she called down to him. She was wearing something silky, something kimono like.

"I know," he agreed. "Something's wrong with me."

"I'll say." She leaned forward, and he caught the scent of oranges. "I think you're used to having your way." That was all she said. She looked at him, as if waiting for him to respond.

"Well, yes," he said.

"Not a man of many words, are you?"

He shook his head.

"Stop looking like a lost puppy. You can come up here if you want. We'll have dinner. We'll talk. And I'll decide later about anything else."

Mike felt his whole body flush with warmth. She was going to see him again. "I happen to be a terrific cook," he said.

"Then get up here," she said with a hint of laughter in her voice. "I'm starving."

Mike nodded, and ran to the house and up the stairs. He was starving too, though he wasn't sure if it was for food…or for Mavis.

Chapter 22

By seven o'clock that evening, Dana's troops had had enough. The twin boys—apparently going through a growth spurt—had nursed until Valerie had passed out in the bathroom. She was seated on the toilet sleeping so deeply, cradling both boys, that Dana didn't have the heart to wake her. She'd simply covered her with a jacket and told Vick to keep an eye on her. When Valerie began to stir, Vick carefully detached the babies, and tenderly tucked them in their car seats.

"Come on, baby," he said to Valerie so softly and with such tenderness that Dana for a moment had a glimpse of the depth of their love for each other.

Valerie opened her eyes, stood up slowly and Vick helped her into her jacket. "Call me," she said sleepily to Dana. "In about three days." She'd turned to Vick and said, "I'm so tired, Vick. I'm never having babies again. Unless we also get a cow to feed them."

"I know, sweetheart," he said and then walked with her outside.

Zach and Ruby had played themselves into a frenzy, and her parents were now packing them up in the car as well.

"They're covered in jam," her dad said. "Why, I bet we could toss them against the wall and they'd stick. Hey, Zach, come here! I want to toss you against a wall."

Her son stared at him. "Gramps. You are *not* doing that. Uh-uh. No way. No how. If you try to do that, I'll shoot you with my laser gun."

"I shot a laser gun once," her dad replied, completely deadpan. "I only shot it once because I'm a very good shot." For a moment Zach looked scared, then his grandpa ruffled his hair. "Come on, kiddos. Let's move 'em out!"

Dana's mom kissed her cheek. "Don't worry. We'll soak them in a bath, stuff them with food, and tuck them in bed. Take your time. Go get a drink or something. Relax a bit. We've got everything under control."

At that point, Ruby threw herself at her grandmother's feet in a terrific tantrum, perhaps finally morphing into the miniature Hulk that her t-shirt promised. All Dana could see was Ruby's red tutu and her blonde hair, and the kicking of tiny red-leotard legs. They waited for a few minutes until the screams became a little more reasonable.

"Okay. Good one, Ruby," Dana's mom said. "Come to Nana now." She bent down and scooped Ruby into her arms.

"Nana, I am not tired," Ruby said defiantly.

"I know."

"I do not want a bath."

"I know."

"I do not want to go to bed."

"I know."

Ruby eyed her grandmother suspiciously. "Then what are you going to do with me at home?"

"I'm going to give you a bath and put you to bed. How does that sound?"

"That sounds good." Ruby snuggled her face against her grandmother.

"We'll see you later," she said to Dana. Dana nodded and blew kisses as her parents finally got them out.

In the kitchen, Jennie and Brent were wiping down the counters. Their mouths were red, so clearly they hadn't been cleaning the entire time. "You guys are terrific. You want to take some chutney with you? It's really good with ham, turkey, pork loin, whatever."

"Hell, yes, we're taking some chutney!" Brent said and grabbed for two of the jars. "Ouch!"

The jars had just been taken out of the canner and were still warm.

Dana wrapped them in a towel. "Give them a couple of weeks. They'll be perfect by Christmas," she said. "And thank you both."

And with that, she had the whole restaurant to herself.

It was quiet.

So deeply quiet.

Dana sat at the counter and looked at her bounty. She'd prepared two different kinds of chutneys and a rich holiday preserve of spiced apples and hints of clove. The restaurant smelled warm and homey and somehow like Christmas.

She reached for a bottle of wine that she'd brought with her for just this moment and poured herself a glass.

Just as she was about to take a well-earned sip, she heard a knock at the front of the restaurant. Then she heard the knocking again. Someone was knocking on the door.

She walked through the kitchen and stopped dead in her tracks. There was a dark silhouette standing outside the window, and he looked like…

Elvis.

Chapter 23

Dana was sure she was hallucinating. Surely, the fumes from all the fruit and sugar and spices had pickled her brain because what else could explain the tall and broad-shouldered Elvis with the little belly standing outside the family diner? And why was he striking a John Travolta Saturday Night Fever pose? With a rose between his lips?

And then it dawned on her. That wasn't Elvis. It was…

The phrase "holy shit" didn't really capture what Dana was feeling. She felt an assortment of things as she shakily reached for the door and opened it. Fear, excitement, a strange mix of sexual attraction and repulsion, a weird calling to touch those sequins, and a fascination with the man's chest hair. Literally. He had like one chest *hair*.

"Theo?" she asked. "Is that…?"

"Well, hello there, pretty lady," he mumbled in a bad Elvis accent. Then he took off his sunglasses and looked at her.

There was a moment or so of perfect awkwardness. A cool breeze swept from the outside straight into the restaurant. She could hear the buzzing of the streetlights. She was certain she could even hear the pounding of blood surging through her body. And then Theo handed her the rose. It was plastic.

"I know this is really weird…" he started.

And then Dana did the only thing she could. Really, she had no choice. She started laughing. "What on earth…?" she started. Then she noticed the bulge in his jumpsuit. That set off a different kind of laughter, one that was more of an excited giggle as she tried to map the shape of the bulge with her mind to determine if it were real or…enhanced. She shook the thought from her mind.

"Come inside," she said finally. "And I want to know just what the hell…how you're here…why on earth…?" Dana couldn't form any sentences. "Did you bring a change of clothes, because I'm not sure I can talk to you in that getup without laughing at you."

Theodore smiled and nodded. "I'm really glad you said that because this jumpsuit really itches. I think I'm allergic to polyester. I might actually be chafing."

"Take it off. I mean, get undressed. I mean, you know, take your clothes off. Change. Uh…" Dana said and then quickly added, "I mean, get comfortable. I have wine, and we can sit and chat and you can explain why you're here." She paused for a moment, looking at him. "I don't need to be freaked out by this, do I?" Dana was certain she didn't. She felt surely there must be a perfectly logical explanation for this…and if at any time she felt threatened, she'd use one of the many defense moves her dad had taught her over the years, with thanks to the National Guard.

"You don't need to be freaked out. I'm they guy who placed that huge order with you. For my store. In Grand Rapids."

Dana really was going to need a drink for this. She's expected to hand over the order to some Spanish chef or something…not a bad Elvis impersonator. Not a man she'd pretended to marry once upon a time under the sparkling magic of Las Vegas.

"Tell me everything, but change first. I don't want to be held responsible for your chafing."

Chapter 24

A few minutes later, they were seated in a little booth, looking at each other. The red vinyl squeaked when they sat, sounding flatulent.

"Excuse me," Dana said and then shrugged. "Ah, the fart joke," she continued, "I just wasn't able to resist."

"You said it before I could." Theodore set his ridiculous, itchy costume in a plastic bag at his feet and was now in his comfortable uniform of corduroy pants and a zip-up sweater. It occurred to him that he really should've thought more about what he was wearing. All he needed was a pair of loafers, and he would've successfully transformed from a bad Elvis to an even worse Mister Rogers. Nobody wanted to sleep with Mister Rogers. Not that he was here to sleep with Dana. Gosh, no. He was just here to talk to her about… He reminded himself that he was a taken man. Very taken. Nearly married. And the final death toll would happen shortly after Christmas.

Theodore cleared his throat. "I thought I'd never see you again," he began. That seemed a safe enough start.

"Yeah," Dana said nodding. "Me too. What happened? How did you find me?"

Theodore could feel himself break out in a sweat. The whole thing was so unbelievable. Coincidences only seemed to happen to other people or in badly plotted films. They didn't happen in real life, and especially *his* real life. "You're not going to believe this…" he said, "but you dropped off a couple of sample jams at my store."

"Your store?" Dana asked, sounding confused.

"Yeah. Foodies. That's my store."

"But I thought you said you owned a store in a metropolitan area…" Dana seemed to be considering that statement, as if she was trying to figure out if Grand Rapids was actually *metropolitan.*

"I do own a store in a metropolitan area. In Detroit. Or the suburbs of Detroit. This store is my second. And you dropped off jam and when I saw the label, I sort of couldn't believe it…"

"And then you placed an enormous order for the jams just so you could meet me," Dana finished for him. Her voice sounded a little sad. Theodore had hoped his actions would flatter her.

"Well, yes and no," Theodore scratched the bridge of his nose. "Yes, I placed an order, and I wanted to meet you, but the jams are really good. My business partner Mike is all for it. We want to highlight them in the store. And I tried to pick up the phone and call you a million times just to talk about the…business opportunities…and then…" Theodore couldn't finish. He'd found that he was suddenly staring at her lips, and he had an image of leaning into her, pressing his body against hers, and the feel of the elevator floating them gently up into the stratosphere as she tilted her head, exposing the lean line of her neck and he kissed her softly. It was an incredible feeling and one that still reverberated within him. When he kissed Sarah, mostly he felt the need for Chapstick. And it had seemed after a moment or two of kissing her, Sarah would glance at her watch, as if willing it to be over.

"And?" Dana asked, wondering why he had just spaced out on her.

Theodore tried to stop thinking about kissing her. He managed to say, "I couldn't call. I don't know. After our little…adventure…in Las Vegas…and the, uh, contact we had and the…wed—…the silly ceremony…a call seemed…"

"Awkward? Phony?" Dana suggested.

"Just *wrong*, I guess," Theodore answered simply. It was a weak explanation he knew, but it was all he had.

"You're right," she said with another laugh. "I much prefer Elvis appearing on my doorstep. I have to say…that's a first." She smiled at him again and immediately he remembered the way his hands felt wound in her hair. "So…we meet again."

"So, we meet again," he echoed.

They sipped their wine.

Dana looked at him, seeming to consider something. "I'm divorced. My husband cheated on me and left me for a woman who is younger and prettier and has firmer breasts, and now they're going to have a baby. I have two kids. They're young. Six and four. Boy and girl. I'm not ready to date. I'm terrified of it. The last time I dated was last century. For real. And I don't like being naked anymore, even in the shower and…" She paused and took a breath. She seemed to give in to the inertia of talking. "When I met you in Las Vegas, I thought I'd never see you again so that's why I was able to be so relaxed."

"And?" Theodore asked, just to be sure there wasn't anything she'd left out…like her blood type or something.

"And I'm really not relaxed now. Not one bit." She ran a hand through her hair. It snagged on what must be some residual jam clumped in her bangs. She exhaled, releasing all the breath from her body, then smiled at him. "You?" she challenged.

Theodore didn't bother thinking before he spoke. He was always thinking, it seemed, measuring everything out, controlling everything he said, especially around Sarah. He just spoke, knowing all along that the real reason he wanted to see Dana had nothing at all to do with business. He just wanted this. To talk to her. Without fear.

"I have a fiancée. Her name is Sarah. I'm supposed to marry her in six weeks, and I can't…I can't stop thinking about you. I didn't mean to kiss you in Vegas or even spend time with you, but I couldn't stop myself. It's why I, at least, stopped from asking you to come into my room…though I wanted to very much. You're very, very desirable." He took a breath and plowed forward. "I don't know what I'm doing anymore. I sort of resigned myself to a life with Sarah, even though she seems to hate me and hate food. I thought I could marry her and then I met you and you reminded me what it was like to laugh and to have fun and to…feel like a man, I guess. I feel awful for kissing you, for pretending to marry you when I'm in a committed relationship, and I also feel like I shouldn't be here. At the same time, talking to you makes me feel…light…even though I could probably lose a few pounds."

They sat in silence for a moment, then Dana said, "Anything else?"

"Well…" he searched for the words. "I wish that I were entirely free, even though you're not ready to date, and I'd probably be a lousy date anyway. I wish I could take you to dinner. I wish…" He couldn't finish. He'd run out of words entirely.

"Oh," Dana said.

"Yep," Theodore replied.

"Okay, then," Dana said. She set her glass of wine down. Theodore mirrored her. Together they stepped away from the booth and stood for just a moment in the dark and empty family diner, a flickering light from outside filtering in.

"Dana?" Theodore asked.

Really, that seemed to be all she needed to hear. Just her name. Theodore didn't try to explain it, or understand it, or process it, or stop it, because after he said her name she just…leapt. Really. She leapt right at him, kissing him as fiercely as one of those mega powerful vacuum cleaners—not that he'd ever actually been kissed by one of those.

Theodore responded. Are you kidding? Of course he responded! And pretty soon their bodies were pressed against each other, and they were rubbing hands through hair and kissing each other.

Chapter 25

"Here," Theodore managed and tried to lay Dana down on the tabletop. The table wobbled threateningly.

"Booth! Booth!" she cried. She laid down on it, or rather fell backwards into the booth, the red vinyl squeaking again and letting out a hiss of air. Theodore fell on top of her. Their legs hung off the side of the booth, Dana's legs bent downward, Theodore practically kneeling to get on top of her, but they didn't care, because they were kissing each other, and nothing felt as good as their kissing felt…except maybe winning the lottery. That would certainly feel good, but no, nothing was a good as the moment they were both trapped in, but willingly trapped. He kissed her neck, her throat, her lips. God, her lips.

She opened to him, parted her mouth, kissed him tenderly and deeply. She ran her hands down the slope of his back, felt the muscles just under the corduroy. God, corduroy was sexy. Why hadn't she known that corduroy was sexy? And a zip-up sweater! Hello, Colin Firth!

Theodore tugged on the top two buttons of her shirt, opening it slightly. He kissed the rise of her breasts, the lacy line of her bra. She smelled good. She tasted good. She was like two mounds of warm, rising bread. Or two scoops of cool, luscious ice cream or… He stopped himself. Now was not the time to think of food! Now was not the time!

He kissed her.

To Dana, Theodore smelled good too. He tasted good…and then…she could feel that bulge in the front of his pants pressing against her, and thank you Jesus, it was not at all enhanced, but 100% real. Dana almost cheered. Instead, she stopped his kisses long enough to whisper, "Do you have a…?"

At first Theodore didn't understand. He was too focused on kissing breast swells. Or the swell of breasts. Or, fuck it, he was kissing the tops of breasts that would lead down to real breasts and possibly to…no, not possibly…*certainly*, those breasts certainly lead down to real nipples. Nipples that he wanted for himself. Now.

"Do you?" Dana asked again.

"Do I what?" he asked.

"You know. Have…a…?"

Then it dawned on him. Oh…did he? Did he have a what did you call it? "Prophylactic?" he said. And then as he did a mental face palm. No one called it a prophylactic. That sounded so clinical, and possibly painful. Oh, why didn't he carry one in his pocket like he did when he was a hopeful teenager? Why? *Why*? He shook his head. Then something else occurred to him. He sat up. "I'm sorry…I can't…"

"I know," Dana breathed. "It's too soon anyway."

Her breathing was heavy, her breasts rising in front of him. "No, I mean…Dana…I'm engaged. I'm in a committed relationship. I can't do this. I can't be here. I can't…"

Dana nodded. She understood. It was strange being on the other side of things, and she suddenly felt as if she could understand why Paul had cheated on her. In all of her life, kissing had never felt this good, and she had never wanted a man as deeply as she wanted Theodore. Right now. She didn't care if it was too early, she didn't care that he was taken, she didn't care that she wasn't really in a good shape for a relationship.

Hormones were raging and like the Body Snatchers, those hormones had taken over her brain. Or possibly replaced her brain with sexual, throbbing organs—that image seemed to cool her down a bit.

"You're taken," she said. "And I'm not ready anyway. And this is foolish."

They looked at each other for a moment, thinking exactly the same thing: that this was all part of that same crazy adventure and that they needed to be sensible…but for some reason, they both told their brains to shut up.

This time, Theodore leapt at Dana. If they hadn't been trapped in a booth, they'd have been rolling all over the restaurant, the way kids roll down steep hills. They kissed and kissed and kissed until they were utterly worn out by their own passion. And by the uncomfortable position of being squished onto a booth, half of their bodies balanced on the floor.

Finally, they came to their senses. Or rather, maybe they'd finally had enough of making out like teenagers in a basement party. The kisses slowed, their breathing steadied, and then they realized they were in a booth, and their muscles were cramping.

"Do you want me to get off you now?" Theodore managed.

"Okay," Dana said.

He stood up, tried to cover up the tent in his pants. She tried not to notice the tent in his pants, but it was hard to miss. You could sleep two in there, maybe with room for a dog.

"It was really nice that you stopped by," she said, hand extended. He reached for her hand, helped her stand up. She smoothed the front of her shirt, buttoned one of the buttons to hide at least some of her cleavage, and tucked a wayward strand of hair behind her ear.

"Dana," he said softly. "We can't ever do that again."

"I know," she said.

"I don't regret it…I just…"

"I know," she said again.

Theodore seemed to consider something. "Can I see you again?"

Dana said the only thing she could think of. "Yes."

Chapter 26

Theodore felt terrible and wonderful at once. On his drive back to Grand Rapids, he could barely focus on staying within the speed limit. If a man could actually be two people at once, Theodore knew how that would feel. On one hand he was ecstatic. Kissing Dana felt exactly right. Just being in the same room with her felt exactly right, so right that he started to accelerate with a rush of endorphins pouring through him…and yet…he was engaged. To Sarah. In a committed relationship. With Sarah. Doomed to a life holding Sarah's arm, wearing what Sarah wanted, eating what Sarah demanded. The thought immediately made him want to put on the brakes.

He knew what he was doing. Kissing Dana was about the connection he felt with her, yes. It was about hormones or pheromones or whatever peculiar magic made a man want to be with a woman, and he was pretty certain it was mutual. It was also something more. It felt like a ritual, almost. A way to break out of the life that he had committed himself to.

Committed himself to. The phrase alone sounded daunting.

Theodore put his blinker on and pulled off to the rest stop that was just ten minutes from his home. It couldn't wait though, and he didn't trust himself to talk to her while driving.

Interesting that after all this time, he still didn't know Sarah's number by heart. He had to look it up in the contacts. She answered after three rings. She didn't even say hello.

"It's late, Theodore. If you want sex or something it's going to have to wait at least another four days. I have my period. And I have a ton of work to do."

"Sarah," he said taking a deep breath. "I'm not making a booty call, or whatever. I'm calling because I need to talk to you."

"We can talk tomorrow. We have an appointment to taste cakes, though I'm on a diet. I suppose you'll have to taste all the cakes and give me detailed descriptions…"

"I have to talk to you tonight." Even as he mouthed the words, he knew it was true. He couldn't wait any longer. He had to tell her the truth about everything. "I can be at your apartment in twenty minutes."

He heard her groan. "I'll meet you at your place," she said. "But I mean it. No sex."

"Believe me," he said. "That's not what this is about."

Chapter 27

When he pulled up to his home in the quiet neighborhood, every house was dark except for his own. Sarah must have turned on every light in the place. Though the house was perfectly nice and located blocks from East Grand Rapids—the wealthy area of town—Sarah was terrified that hooligans would target Theodore's place and steal everything inside it, including Sarah. If hooligans hadn't known about the unassuming brick house before, they certainly would now. It almost looked as if it was on fire.

Sarah had parked on the street, which was interesting to him. It was almost as if she was prepared for what was coming.

He parked his car and walked inside. If he'd had any doubt before, within minutes, all doubt was erased.

Sarah stood in front of him, rage radiating off of her. "Who is Dana Delight? Are you fucking a porn star?"

He flinched at her vulgarity. "No, Sarah, that's not what this is—" He didn't have time to finish.

"I know what this is about. You suddenly have cold feet about our wedding. Just stop it. You're not getting out of it. I've got almost the whole thing planned. And in just two more weeks, we're having Thanksgiving at the country club with my family, and I want them to know that everything is under control. So, please, just get off your chest what you need to and then shut up about everything."

Her every word was like a barbed wire digging in to his flesh. He sat down at the dining room table. He didn't feel angry or fear or sadness. He just felt numb. And that wasn't right. "Sarah, I can't marry you," he began.

"Get over yourself!" she said. Then she tried to lighten the mood and laughed a little, while sitting across from him. "Sheesh. You're like a woman sometimes, I swear. What is this issue? If you need sex so much, let's go upstairs and I'll…wank you or whatever. Just stop being so emotional."

"That's just it!" Theodore said. "I don't feel emotional about you, Sarah. I don't feel anything. Nothing. That's cold and harsh, but it's true."

There was silence.

"I gave up on the whole fairytale romance thing ages ago, Theodore. We both know we aren't emotional people. We'll get married and move out of this place and into East and then everything will be great. We are the picture perfect couple. Just stop being so glum. I told you I'd take care of everything."

What was meant to appease him only deepened his certainty. He spoke slowly and tried to fill his words with confidence. "I don't love you. I can't marry you. I won't marry you. This is over. You, me, we only appear like the picture perfect couple. And the thing is, I don't want perfect. Perfection is for magazines. I want real life."

He could hear the pounding of his heart. He wondered if Sarah could hear it too.

"I don't love you either," she said finally, but it wasn't with fury this time; it was with the softness of admitting the truth. "I thought we were above that. I don't think real love happens anyway."

For the first time in a long while, Theodore caught a glimpse of Sarah's vulnerability. He loved her a little bit for that realness. As quickly as it appeared, though, it vanished. He saw her cheeks redden as the full impact of his words hit her. She finally believed him. They were done.

She stood and said, "I've wasted two years on you, Theodore! Two! Two years of my life and my beauty. And you know what? You don't deserve me. You're not good enough. You're boring and you snore and you have a small penis and… And I hate that you wear sweaters. So fuck you."

With that, she stormed out, slamming the door behind her.

Almost immediately she stormed back in. "And I want to get all the things out of your sorry excuse for a house immediately. I don't want anyone stealing my things."

Theodore thought for a moment; even this seemed to be a significant sign that he was only now able to notice. "You don't have anything here, Sarah, unless you want to take a spare toothbrush. You hate this house and you said you didn't want to leave anything until we were married and could buy a new house."

Sarah just glared at him—her color deepening to a frightening plum color. "Mother fucker!" she screamed again and then re-stormed out.

Theodore waited until her car screeched away and he could no longer hear the motor before he allowed himself to breathe.

Now what? What did he do? Did that just happen? He knew by the lightness in his chest that it had happened, and he did just break up with her. There would be phone calls to make. Explanations. Cancellations. A whole stack of tidying up the end of their relationship, for he had no doubt that he would not go back to her. Something between them, that fragile connection, had just broken when she'd mentioned his sweaters. But all of that…all of the tidying could wait.

For now, he would just sit in the silence and breathe.

Chapter 28

Mike couldn't stop looking at her. The moonlight washed over her smooth skin, highlighting the curve of her hip, the soft rise of her breasts.

"I know you're staring at me," Mavis said, even though her eyes were closed.

He reached over and touched a soft strand of silky hair.

"I'm twenty years older than you."

"I know."

"I have grandchildren."

"I know."

"I can't have children anymore. I'm way past that."

"I don't need my own kids."

Mike couldn't believe how calm he felt. Like he was talking directly from his soul.

Mavis opened her eyes and sat up, exposing her breast fully to him. "I've been married four times. One of them had a heart attack. Two of them had affairs. And one of them was gay. I'm not looking for forever, but you have to know that if you pull any shit with me…if we are in a committed relationship and you start cheating on me, that's it. I won't even have a conversation with you. You'll find all your bags packed, and you'll be out the door. I'm not looking for forever, but I am looking for an intense now."

Mike smiled. For the first time in years, it seemed like he could relax. "I can give you an intense now."

"I'm counting on it," she said. "How about right this moment?"

With the moonlight falling over her in a strip of light blue and her lying fully exposed to him, Mike didn't need to wait for a second invitation. He kissed her slowly. They didn't need to rush. They had all the time in the world.

Chapter 29

"Mom! Mom! Mom!" Ruby screamed from her bedroom. "Can I get up now?"

Dana tried to open her eyes and look at her alarm clock next to her. Everything was blurry at first and then she saw the red numbers that read 4:35AM.

"It's too early!" she groaned.

"But I'm awake!" Ruby screamed from her bedroom. "Mom! I'm awake! And I want to do a craft project!"

Dana rubbed her eyes and fumbled out of bed. If she didn't get up right now, Ruby would go into hysterics and then wake up Zach and she'd have *two* screaming, hysterical kids on her hand.

It's a phase, she told herself. Ruby is going through a phase. Though this phase of waking up when the world was still dark was getting very, very old. Dana wanted to blame the time change, but she thought that

Ruby's perpetual early-birdness might be a biorhythm thing, and it was very hard to fight against chemistry.

"Coming!" Dana said, stepped slowly out of bed, fumbled for her pink bathrobe and slipped into it.

"You're awake, huh?" she said, moments later, standing in her daughter's doorway.

"Yep," Ruby said. She didn't just sound awake. She sounded ready for world domination. She was kneeling in her bed, clad in a purple nightgown decorated with owls. Her short blonde hair stood up in three different places. "Will you carry my stuff?"

"What stuff?" asked Dana.

Ruby motioned behind her. "All of it."

Dana nodded. She was too tired to try to reason with Ruby. And, frankly, all the kissing last night had knocked out any will to argue. "All of it" consisted of twelve stuffed animals, a puzzle, some dress up clothes, her favorite Elnono and an O Magazine. Ruby liked the picture of Oprah on it. Sometimes she just carried the magazine around.

"Come on, kiddo, let's go downstairs. And be quiet. Do not wake your brother."

"Okay, Ma. I'll be quiet like a mouse," her daughter agreed. "Did you know mouses aren't really quiet? They squeak all the time. My best friend Maggie told me that. She has mouses at her house."

"Good to know," Dana said. "No more play-dates there. Now, let's go downstairs. You can work at the dining room table."

Ruby, thankfully, agreed. While settling Ruby in for her arts and craft project of putting beads onto pipe cleaners to make bracelets, Dana thought about last night. And she thought about the nights to come. Could she do this? Could she date again? She didn't know how to date. Not with two kids. How did single moms do that?

Clearly, there were still some pent up sexual feelings within her, so at least she wasn't dead in that way. After Paul had left her, she'd seriously wondered if she'd ever feel passionate again.

Dana got the coffee brewing. It had been over a year now that she'd been on her own, but she could still feel the echoes of pain that this last year had left on her. First, the realization that her husband had fallen in love with another woman, but deeper than that was the understanding that they hadn't loved each other for a very long time. They'd become roommates over the years, especially since Ruby was born. All the things that a married couple was supposed to enjoy had slipped away from them. Things like laughter, conversation, and eventually even sex.

Part of the reason kissing Theodore felt so good was, well, because she was attracted to him, yes, and she liked what little she knew of him…but it was also because for the first time in a very long time, Dana felt connected to her own body. She'd been a wife and mother for so long now, that she'd forgotten she was also a woman.

Maybe that's what had happened with Paul. Maybe when he met Alyssa he felt like the man he should have been. It made her forgive him just a little bit.

She sat at the table with Ruby and flipped through a magazine. The coffee burbled happily in the kitchen. Ruby concentrated on the beads by sticking out her tongue and putting each bead on the pipe cleaner with great focus.

Last year, in this house, at this very table, when the kids were sleeping, Paul had said to her, "Dana, I just can't do this anymore. And it isn't because I've fallen in love with someone else, although that's part of it. I think maybe, it's possible that you and I were never right for each other from the start."

She'd wanted to slap him then, and she had yelled at him. And cried. And screamed. He'd listened stoically and then when he felt she'd had her say, he grabbed his suitcase and left. He'd come back later to see the kids and taken them out to dinner, and eventually, he had rented an apartment for them. But that was the end of their marriage.

Dana thought it was the end of her. She'd been terrified. How was she supposed to take care of two kids on her own? How did she pay the mortgage? And now, when one of the kids was having a meltdown, she had no one to turn to for help. Every scraped knee, every disappointment, every time the kids threw up or needed something, the responsibility fell entirely to Dana.

This constant need from her children consumed every waking moment of Dana's, not just life but, existence. Everything she did, she did to take care of them. She tried to make the split with their dad natural and not threatening. She picked up waitressing jobs to cover additional bills. She decided not to fight Paul in terms of custody or what he was willing to pay in child support, because she didn't want to put her kids through that. She accepted his decisions, and then she did what she had to to survive. And she'd done it. She'd made money. She paid the mortgage. She took care of the kids. And now she was starting a business of her own.

The coffee gurgled. "Mom!" Ruby said, not looking up from her jewelry making. "Your coffee's ready. Can you get me something to drink?"

"You want coffee?" Dana joked.

"Mom…" Ruby said, finally looking up at her and rolling her eyes. Dana smiled, thinking of how Ruby might look when she was a teenager. It was the expression of an exasperated daughter dealing with her mom. The same expression Dana had used on her mother, and still used with her mother at times. "I want juice. And some toast. Maybe some apple. But don't cut it. I want the apple big."

"Okay…okay," Dana said, surrendering.

She went into the kitchen and busied herself with her morning tasks.

It was dark out and quiet. Upstairs, her son slept peacefully. The heater clicked on. Her house smelled of coffee. She could hear the gentle clink of the beads on the table as Ruby threaded her pipe cleaner. Soon, her son would wake up and the day would be filled with laughter and frenetic activity and tantrums and making food together and toys spilled all over the house as if a tornado had swept through her home.

She poured cream into a mug and then the coffee over it. It swirled and went from a deep brown to a caramel color. She sipped her coffee. Her eyes filled with tears. How on earth was she supposed to open her heart and share all of this wonder with someone again?

In that way, kissing Theodore had been safe. He was taken and that was that. The kiss was a momentary weakness. She took it as a gift from the universe reminding her that she could feel passion again. But love? Could she feel love again? Love was another story…and she wasn't yet ready to find out.

Chapter 30

Theodore and Mike were in Eastown, the artsy little section of Grand Rapids where you'd see college students, young families with babies, and baby boomers all dressed in the same uniform of skinny jeans, bad sweaters, knit hats, and tennis shoes. In Eastown, everyone was a hipster. Even the dogs. There were small coffee shops, the roads were paved in brick, and everything felt like it was still nestled safely in the 1970s. There were also three breakfast joints within two blocks of each other, to balance out the number of bars in the small neighborhood of Grand Rapids.

They were seated in the window of Wolfgang's looking at the street and the activity going on around them. At 6:00AM on a Sunday, one would think there wouldn't be any activity going on outside, especially since with the time change it was still dark outside, but Eastown was slowly waking up. Cars drove past the restaurant, a college kid on a bike wearing a huge puffy jacket and a hat with ear flaps sped by, and a couple kissed under Yesterdog's awning, either just going home together, or leaving one another to start the day.

Their breakfast was a business meeting, of course, since the store was having its grand opening tomorrow. But even with a stack of things to get through, there was still time to talk over their enormous breakfast skillets.

Mike had taken one look at Theodore and said, "You look like shit," by way of a greeting. "Let's get food first and you can tell me what's going on over that."

Theodore nodded.

So as they waited for their breakfasts, they had their regular business chit chat covering last minute details and their plan for the final moments before the opening, but as soon as the waitress delivered their gigantic breakfasts, Mike said, "Spill it."

"I met Dana last night," Theodore said as he sprinkled hot sauce over his eggs/potatoes/sausage/veggies skillet. He wasn't sure where he was going to start. Did he start with Dana or with Sarah? It was almost too soap opera to think about.

"Your wife from Vegas?" Mike asked after taking a gigantic bite of eggs and potatoes.

"Yes. And stop it. She's not my wife. It was just a joke and a stupid thing we did."

"I know you didn't fill out any formal paperwork, but in some cultures, if you stand before Elvis and make an oath of marriage, then you are bound forever."

"What cultures?"

"Any culture who believes the one truth that Elvis is King."

Theodore laughed. "Well, yeah, okay then. So. I saw my wife last night."

Mike nodded, smeared some butter on his toast. "How did it go?"

Theodore felt a rush of heat flood over his body and the faint stirring of attraction…not for Mike, though he was a handsome enough fellow, but at the mere suggestion of Dana. He had an instant flash of unbuttoning her shirt, the swell of what promised to be two perfect breasts, and how she tasted when he kissed her. Then he immediately thought of an obese hairy man in a showgirl's bikini. He had to do something quick or he wouldn't be able to walk out of the restaurant. This was how he controlled himself. Obese Hairy Man in a Bikini had helped him for years. "It went good.'"

Mike nodded. "Uh, huh. You slept with her, didn't you?"

"Mike. Come on! Sarah, remember? Engaged? Me? I did not sleep with her." Theodore wanted to leave it at that, but Mike was chewing his toast with a look that said "sure right". Theodore didn't even know one could chew his toast that way, but apparently one could. "I just kissed her." More chewing. "Okay. Enough, Mike. Stop it. I kissed her for an hour or so."

Mike looked at him strangely. It was as if he were Jane Goodall studying the behavior of a foreign primate species. "You kissed her for an hour or so, but didn't sleep with her? Do you have ED? Erectile Dysfunction, because there's a pill for that."

Theodore was about to respond, but Mike kept going. "I had ED once. Couldn't get it up. I got those pills and everything. Turns out it wasn't that I didn't want to have sex anymore, I just didn't want to be married. That was wife number two. When we broke up, my ED was totally gone. But, yeah, so was most of my money in the divorce."

Mike seemed to think on that for a while. "I don't know why you're so obsessed with getting married. You're engaged to one woman and play at being married to another. Marriage is serious business."

Theodore shook his head and kept eating. If he'd thought there'd be any judgment from Mike, a lengthy harangue about how could he kiss another woman when he was engaged, he was wrong. Mike didn't judge anyone. He didn't have it in him.

"There's more," Theodore confessed. "I sort of completely broke it off with Sarah." He waited for Mike to show some reaction, but he just kept chewing away. "There's no more wedding. We're through. I don't love her the way you should love the woman you're going to marry."

Mike's response was a simple shrug and a nod. "Now what?" he asked. "Are you seeing Dana again?"

"No! I mean I just broke up with Sarah. Don't you think there should be like a period of mourning, or some kind of waiting time so that I don't come off looking like a complete prick?"

"You're either half a prick or a complete prick in this. If I were you, and I had those two choices, I'd choose being a complete prick every time. Besides, Sarah is so not the one for you. She'd carry your balls in her purse. You'd be like one of those creepy little dogs that people dress up in raincoats. You're better off."

Theodore considered that. "Okay. Yes. I am seeing Dana again. To talk business. Business!"

"When?"

"Tonight, actually."

"Tonight." Mike looked quizzically at him again. "And you just saw her yesterday?"

Theodore nodded.

Mike tossed his napkin on the table. It rather looked like he was throwing down the gauntlet. "Man, what are you doing? You're going against all the Man Rules."

"Man Rules?" Theodore asked although he had a feeling where this might be heading.

Mike leaned closer and whispered intently. "You know the Man Rules. I know the Man Rules. Everyone knows the Man Rules, we just don't talk about the Man Rules. It's like Fight Club that way, except there's no fighting. You're the man. You pay for the first dinner. She's supposed to at least offer to pay. When you kiss, you kiss her first. In fact, go back. You call her first. You ask her out first. The Man Rules state that the Man must do the act of pursuing or your relationship is doomed. You kiss her first. Did you kiss her first last night?"

Theodore thought about it. It had felt more mutual than that, but when he replayed the scene… "She kissed me." Then he immediately envisioned Hairy Man in Bikini one more time.

"She kissed you! See? You're doomed. And then you're supposed to not call her for like three days. At least three days. You ignore her. That gets her all obsessing about whether or not she's into you and gives her time to go out with her girlfriends and analyze everything to death. Then in three days you call her and ask her out again, but only give her one, maybe two, options as to time. Those are the Man Rules. There are more, but I just don't have the energy to tell you." He finished his monologue by scooping up another enormous bite of eggs.

"Tell me, how many times have you been married?" Theodore asked.

"Three."

"Exactly. Your Man Rules are shit."

Mike seemed to consider this. "Well played, Theodore. Well played."

"I'm going out with her tonight," Theodore said, tossing his napkin on the table. He could throw down the gauntlet with the best of them.

"Well, if you're going out tonight, then we need to head over to Foodies. We've got some serious work to do before the opening tomorrow."

Theodore agreed. They motioned to the waitress for their bills. It occurred to Theodore, as he sat there with Mike drinking coffee and watching the city wake up around him, that for living a pretty controlled and boring life, suddenly things felt like they were about to get exciting.

Somehow, Dana had helped him discover his Elvis within. He rather liked the effect Elvis was having on him.

Chapter 31

Dana's morning passed quickly. She fed the kids, cleaned a little, checked her email. There was one from Theodore that said, "I really enjoyed re-meeting you. And…uh…yes. Looking forward to tonight." Dana had laughed at that. Even in his emails he was slightly awkward.

After lunch, her sister and her boys came over. They were going to watch Ruby and Zach so she could have a "meeting" with Theodore. Dana vowed to herself that they would only talk spices and not actually *be* spicy. He was taken and that made him off limits. And Dana wasn't ready for anything other than a little fun in Vegas, and a little old school make out session last night. But it would end right there.

"Oh, yeah." Valerie said. "Mom and Dad will be here in a few minutes."

Dana gulped. "What? What do you mean Mom and Dad are coming over? Why would they come over? Wait. Wait! Did you tell them I have a *date*?"

"I maybe mentioned that, yes, you have a date tonight," Valerie said, standing in the kitchen with Dana waiting for the late afternoon coffee to finish up. The twins were in the front room with Ruby and Zach. Valerie had set the twins up in the little bouncy seats, and Zach and Ruby were performing a puppet show of sorts for them.

"It isn't a date though," Dana affirmed. "He's engaged. It's business."

"Uh, huh," Valerie said, with a tone that said "riiight".

Dana breathed deeply. Maybe she should cancel the whole thing. It was just tempting disaster, wasn't it? If she could be so attracted to him dressed as Elvis, and then wearing a pullover sweater, imagine what he could do to her if he wore a suit. She tried to clear her head by focusing on the bits and pieces of the show her kids were creating for Valerie's babies in the front room.

Zach said, "Okay, Ruby, I will use the Star Wars action figures, and you can use the stuffed animals. And when the stuffed animals come in, then I will use my laser beams and cut off their heads."

Ruby cried, "Noooo! Not the stuffed animals!"

"There's no blood, Ruby. It's just pretend. I'm not really going to cut their heads off."

"Will there be blood?"

"No. It's just pretend."

Then Dana heard the play start with "I'm cutting off your head!" and then Ruby crying, "Look at all the blood!"

Good, kid friendly entertainment for babies.

"God," Dana breathed. "This is getting out of control. *You're* here. My kids are here. Your kids are here. And our parents are coming. It feels like some freaky prom date, only I've got children. They aren't staying, right?"

Valerie shrugged. "I'm sorry, Dana. The truth is, whether or not you feel like this is a date, for us, it is. Or it has the potential to be. You're a single mom, and we need to look out for you. Protect you. And if we happen to scare the bejeezus out of this Theo dude so that he doesn't take advantage of you, well…" She held up her hands as if to say "there's nothing I can do about that".

"You guys are protecting my honor. Again, weird prom feeling. I'm not fourteen years old."

"Tell Dad that," Valerie said. "He… Well, maybe it's better I don't tell you."

"Is he wearing his fatigues?"

Valerie nodded soberly.

"Oh, God," Dana breathed again. So this was how it was going to be. Even though it wasn't a real date, she told herself, it gave her a glimpse of the future. Dating as a single mom promised to be a nightmare. Gone were the hours of sitting in a bath and shaving your legs and armpits and anything else that could possibly be kissed and/or fondled. She would say goodbye to spending an hour doing her hair and makeup, and the luxury of trying on a dozen different outfits. Dating when you were a mom meant you hoped to God you had time for a shower and that you could find a shirt without a stain on it. And it meant, apparently for Dana, that the man she was going out with was going to have to meet her entire family and possibly pass a hazing ritual.

That's when she started laughing.

"This could only happen to me," she said.

"Better you than me," Valerie said, reaching for the coffee as soon as it had stopped running. "I don't know how I'd handle dating again. Although with my enormous boobs, I think I'd be very popular."

"You'd be totally popular. And thank you for that. The whole idea of being a single mom terrifies me, but at least I'm not still lactating anymore."

Valerie nodded. "Remember when we used to talk about boys when we were teenagers? Remember Kenny? Oh, we wanted Kenny so bad."

"You wanted Kenny so bad."

"So did you. You wrote 'I Heart Kenny' on your folder at school."

"I was talking about Kenny Rogers," Dana said smugly.

"You were not. You were talking about Kenny Sanders. You know what he does now?"

Dana was afraid to ask. "What?"

"He's a drag queen. Her name is Delia." Valerie laughed. "It's too funny how life changes, isn't it? When we were kids we were so worried about dating, and then we got married and had kids, and now you're worried about dating again, and I'm worried about when my nipples are going to go back to their normal size. And isn't it disturbing that I can now talk with you about my nipples and I don't feel the least bit uncomfortable?"

"That's called growing up," Dana said. "And it happened when we weren't looking."

At that point the twins both started crying. "Oh, sheesh," Valerie said, reaching for the bra strap that would free her breasts. "Even mention the word nipples and the boys suddenly want them."

"I don't think they'll ever grow out of that," Dana said.

"My point exactly. Still. Life is surprising. Just ask Delia." With that, Valerie went into the living room to nurse her babies.

Dana smiled to herself. As scary as all of this was, her new side business of making and selling jams and chutneys, and the idea of dating…it was also a lot of fun.

Chapter 32

Mike said his goodbyes to Theodore and kept up his Big Man act until Theodore was far out of sight. Over breakfast, he'd almost cracked and told Theodore that he was in serious trouble with his heart. Not health wise, of course. More like emotion wise. He couldn't stop thinking about Mavis, and not in the way that he used to think about other women. He thought about the way she laughed, a throaty sexy laugh that tickled him in some way. And before coming to breakfast with Theodore, Mike and Mavis had sat at her kitchen table, both of them in silky kimonos drinking coffee and watching the sunrise.

Him. Mike Sparrow. In a silk kimono. Talking about the rosy color of the morning. And he'd never felt better.

He grabbed his car keys and headed for Foodies. He had to do something with his time, but already in his mind, he was counting down the minutes when he could see her again. He'd told Theodore all about the Man Rules, but in truth he knew that when it came to true love, the Man Rules were pointless. He didn't care who called who first or how long it had been or anything. As soon as he could, he'd talk to her again.

Something funny was going on within him. He rather liked it.

Chapter 33

After the kids reenacted old SpongeBob SquarePants cartoons for the babies, and the boys were then nursed into a satisfied coma, Dana cooked up some quick crepes for dinner.

"Crepes? For dinner?" asked Ruby.

Dana nodded. It was a quick recipe and one she knew by heart: put two eggs, 1 ¼ cups of milk, 1 cup of flour and a pinch of salt in a food processor. Blend. Cook crepes in massive amounts of butter and top with her homemade jam. Serve up a side of bacon with it, and the kids were in some kind of bacon heaven.

"Is this backward day?" asked Zach. "It must be backward day if we're having breakfast for dinner." He seemed to think about it. "Actually, it can't be backward day because then I would've had a sandwich in the morning time and in the morning time I ate…what did I eat?"

"We made smoothies."

"Exactly," Zach agreed. "Yogurt smoothies. But then I also had a turkey sandwich so maybe it is backward day."

"I don't know if things are exactly backward but, sure. Dinner is backward."

As soon as Dana had agreed, Zach didn't hesitate. "Then I want ice cream."

"I want ice cream too," Ruby said while coloring a picture of Strawberry Shortcake. "It's backward day."

Dana heard Valerie call from the upstairs where she was changing the boys' diapers. "I want ice cream too."

There were times when you just didn't fight with the masses. Dana scooped the ice cream into dishes, including one for herself. She glanced at the clock. In two more hours, Theodore was going to knock on her door again. And this time he was taking her out. To talk business. She had to keep reminding herself of that because she didn't want… Well. She didn't want to be like her Paul's Alyssa. Not that Alyssa had stolen Paul or anything, and he certainly wasn't without blame, but Dana just didn't want to be the type of woman who broke up someone else's relationship.

She focused her attention. Where would they go? What would they talk about? She was pretty sure he was safe because she and Valerie had Googled his name to death and run it through a police watch list. He seemed to be a decent, hard-working guy. But now that she was actually going out with him and not, say, standing at an altar with him and saying, "I sure do!" while smacking gum, or laying spread eagle beneath him on a red vinyl booth…well, how was she supposed to act? Did they high-five when he came to the door? Did they talk in deep, sophisticated voices about projected earnings and her business plan?

Dana's mind was drifting all over the place. All of this felt like practice-dating, and it scared her to death. It was too complicated! When a real date happened, what did she tell the kids? Was she supposed to keep her dating life entirely secret from them? Wouldn't they be injured emotionally somehow if they saw her go out with a man who wasn't their dad? And what would they think of her leaving with Theodore when everyone else was treating it like a date? What if they understood that but they developed an immediate attachment for Theodore and didn't understand that he wasn't interested in her that way because he wasn't allowed to be? How would she explain it to her kids? She'd wanted to keep even this meeting with Theodore a secret, but something inside her had resisted. Why?

She didn't want to lie. Not to anyone else, and especially not to herself.

The truth then: she felt like there was some connection between her and Theo, something she didn't understand. To be honest, she wanted to find out if it was real or just imagined.

If she was going to date again, if she was going to try and open her heart a little bit to another man, then she'd make a vow to herself: she would be one hundred percent authentic. If she didn't like something or agree with something, she'd say that. If she wasn't having fun, she wouldn't pretend she was. When she thought back on dating Paul, even in the beginning, she had blurred so many of the edges off of what was important to her, that she'd actually become a different person. She would no longer do that. She was Dana Kupiac, a woman with a lot of roles. And part of who she was lived in this house. She was willing to date, but only if the man she was dating knew that she was a single mom and that her two kids were the most important things in her life. She was, as they say, a package deal. He had to know up front that she could go out and have fun, but she had serious responsibilities.

Dana wasn't looking for anyone to take care of her or her kids. She didn't even know that she was actually actively looking for anything… But Theodore's invitation to see him again had been hard to resist. Almost as hard to resist as kissing him. And in his email he had also hinted that there was something he wanted to tell her. Something important. It didn't sound business-related.

She smelled something burning and looked down at the crepe. Her first crepe was black around the edges and burning. "Oh, shoot," she murmured.

Valerie came into the kitchen, sniffing. "Whoa!" she said. "Step away from the stove. You should not be cooking at a time like this. You, go get ready. Shave something. I'll cook. The kids are eating their ice cream."

Dana smiled, nodded, and released her control of the crepe cooking. "Didn't you want ice cream first?"

"Dana, I finished that ice cream in like two bites. I'm an overtired stay-at-home mom to two perpetually nursing boys. I've learned to eat in like three seconds. Tops. Go upstairs. Go crazy. Take a shower."

"There is a special place in heaven for you," Dana said and kissed her sister's cheek.

Valerie scraped out the crepe and began washing the pan. "Yeah? Tell that to my boys when they're starting to date, and I show their girlfriends naked baby pictures."

Chapter 34

Foodies was ready. *They* were ready. Theodore looked around the store and he was…what? Astounded? Proud? Happy? He was happy. The store had deep mahogany floors—made of Pergo flooring—and shelves in the same toasted brown color. Little star-like lights hung from the ceiling. There were wine racks in the back stocked with everything from the $7 Australian blend to $350 French indulgences. The deli case was stocked with gourmet cheeses, dips, and side salads. There was a special case devoted just to truffles and chocolates, provided by a local chocolatier.

Mike and Theodore also stocked gourmet sandwiches, made fresh in the morning, for the array of business people. There was an espresso machine and two small bistro tables with chairs at the front of the store. There were aisles of chips and specialty food items to make anything from Indian to Japanese to Cajun cooking. And peppered around the store were displays of crackers, cheese, and Dana's Delights. Theodore had included her product in a variety of gift baskets. For the opening ceremony they had door prizes, the press coming to interview them and local foodies, and wine ready to pour.

There was nothing left to do today.

Mike clapped him on the back. "This is a good one," he said. "I'm going to have a hard time heading back to Detroit. I think I like this store better."

"You sure it's the store you like or that seventy-year-old woman you're seeing?" Theodore joked.

"She's actually just fifty-eight. And she's hot. Like Sophia Loren hot. And she says she doesn't want any more kids so, yeah. I'm sorta liking her."

Theodore smiled. "You do like her, don't you?"

"Three marriages to perfectly beautiful, pert women, and this one…she's a grandmother, a super-smart attorney, she can beat me in cards and arm wrestling, and I just can't stop thinking about the next time I get to see her." Mike looked around the empty store. "I didn't mean to say any of that out loud."

"I know. It's totally okay." Theodore adjusted some bags of root chips (seasoned with rosemary) on the shelves, though the chips really didn't need adjusting. "I think we're ready."

Mike nodded. "Yeah. Let's hope we're a hit."

At that point they looked out the window to see a large woman in a red jacket approaching. "Ah!" Theodore said. "Meet our new employee. Her name is Angelique. But don't let that fool you. She's a demon."

Angelique opened the door on Theodore's last comment. "You bet your ass I'm a demon. And if anyone tries to steal a sandwich or touch my ass, I will lift them over my head and toss them out the door. I am *not* joking." She walked over to Mike and shook his hand, after which Mike massaged his fingertips.

"Hello, little man," Angelique said to Theodore. "You ready to train me? That's the only time you'll hear me say that. I intend to manage this place eventually, so after today I plan on giving the orders. That okay with you?"

Strangely, it was. "That's what I hired you for," he agreed. After his meeting with her on the street, Angelique had called him up for her free bottle of wine and slid him her resume. She was quite the saleswoman.

"Okay then," she said, smacking her hands together with an eager clap. "Let's get started. And what time is it that you need to leave for that date of yours?"

He looked at his watch. "In an hour and a half."

Angelique took off her jacket, exposing a sequined sweater dress that clung to her every curve. "Okay. That gives you one hour to train me, and me a half hour to give you some pointers on how to treat a woman…because if our first meeting on the street is any indication of how you approach a fine woman, then you have some serious issues we need to address." With that, she turned and walked to the back of the store looking for the closet.

Mike turned to Theodore, his expression making him look dumbfounded. "I love her," he said. "If it doesn't work out between me and my landlady, I'm going to ask Angelique to marry me."

They heard her response from the back of the store, "You can ask me, but I'll say no. I'm already married. Her name is Rachel. We have a house and two kids. And if you think I'm tough, she will kick your little ass if you try to put the moves on me."

Mike gulped then said, "I'm really hoping it works out with my landlady."

Chapter 35

By 6:30, Dana was ready. She was wearing a nice pair of jeans that hugged her in the right places and didn't produce that disconcerting fat roll at the top of the waist. She'd chosen a sturdy but feminine bra that helped her breasts present the illusion of defying gravity while not threatening to poke one's eye out. It was a fine line, sometimes. Mostly, the bra put her breasts back where they belonged. Over the shape-shifting bra, she'd put on a nice gray sweater with a cowl neck.

Such an ugly word, she thought. Cowl. Cowl neck. It sounded like that dangly thing on a rooster.

At any rate, she wore a gray sweater with a soft neckline. She wore her hair down. The gray of the sweater enriched the brown of her eyes, and the deep chestnut of her hair. Valerie had insisted she take a little extra time to put on actual makeup, so Dana had lined her eyes and tried to make them a little smoky. She hoped her eyes looked smoky and not like she'd been hit by a ball.

To complete the look, she put on a strappy pair of heels that she hadn't worn since… She tried to remember if she'd ever worn them. She'd bought them sometime before finding out she was pregnant with Zach, and the shoes had been hanging out in the closet ever since. They were ridiculously tall and beyond that…they were *red.* Still, they made her look taller and thinner and she felt just a little bit sexy wearing them. She decided it was high time she let those wild red shoes out of the closet. They'd earned it.

She took a deep breath. She felt ridiculous. It wasn't as if this were an actual date. Theodore was taken. Very taken. This was just a practice date…for when the real thing happened. Although, really, she shouldn't even think of this as a practice date. This was, then, a mutually beneficial business meeting. That's right. There was nothing more going on here. She checked herself in the mirror again, frowned, bent over and adjusted her boobs. Nothing more she could do.

"All right," she said when she reached the bottom of the stairs. "How do I look?"

Zach, Ruby, Valerie and the babies all sat on the couch, waiting.

"Come out here and walk around for us," Valerie said.

"Yeah, Mom," Ruby said. "Walk around and stuff."

Dana walked back and forth on the rug. Actually, she wobbled more than walked. It would take her a little practice to get used to the shoes.

Zach studied her, his eyes squinting while he focused. "Turn around," he said.

She spun.

Ruby said, "Mom, you look like a princess."

Zach's face scrunched. "No, she doesn't, Ruby. A princess wears pinks and girly stuff and a pointy hat."

"Not all princesses," Ruby said, her lower lip pouting, arms crossed over her chest. "Some princesses don't wear hats."

"Enough, kiddos," Dana said. "Thank you for saying I look like a princess, Ruby. And Zach…it's okay if that's what she thinks. What do you think I look like?"

Zach considered it. "You look the same as you always look. You look pretty."

Well, that comment was enough to make Dana's eyes threaten to spill tears and mess up all her makeup.

Just then there was a knock at the door.

"Oh!" Valerie said, jumping up off the couch. "Go look busy. I'll answer it."

"Mom's date is here! Mom's date is here!" Zach and Ruby said jumping up and down.

"Calm down everyone! This is not a big deal. This is not a date! It's a mutually…beneficial…business meeting." Her kids and Valerie looked at her. They all blinked. "I'm just having dinner with a friend."

The knock repeated.

"Whatever." Valerie pushed Dana to the stairs. "Up!" she whispered and the knocking repeated again.

Dana ran up the stairs and into the bathroom. Date or not, she was a nervous wreck. She wanted to look good. She needed to feel good. She wasn't prepared for this! It was far better to stay home and do a facial than to brave the outside world and have dinner with a man she couldn't help but imagine naked. And on top of her. She needed to clear her head. What could she do? What *should* she do? She looked in the mirror.

Dammit! She looked old. Puffy. She had wrinkles around her eyes, and dark circles which were not smoky at all, no, not smoky. She looked like she had allergies, and her sleek brown hair was threatening to frizz uncontrollably.

She tried not to listen to Valerie open the door, but she heard everything nonetheless.

To Dana's surprise, it wasn't Theodore's voice she heard, but her father's. "Where is this potential new boyfriend!" her father boomed. "I want to know who he is, what his intentions are, and has he ever served in the military!"

"Ralph, ixnay on the military-ay," her mom said.

"I don't believe in ixnay-ing anything. It hurts my prostate. Now, where are the kiddos?"

Dana could hear Ruby and Zach attacking their grandparents. "Nana! Papa!" Ruby cried. "Zach says mom doesn't look like a princess, and I say she does," Dana heard as she came down the stairs.

Her dad watched her walking and smiled up at her. "Of course, she looks like a princess," he said, and then added a little more loudly for Zach's benefit, "in the Federation Army."

"Hi, Dad and Mom," Dana said and kissed their cheeks. She'd so been hoping Theodore would've arrived by now, and they'd be safely on their way to the restaurant. If he'd only been a few minutes early, he could've avoided the sucking vortex that was her family. Why? Why had she agreed to let him pick her up here, in the heart of chaos?

"Dana, you look gorgeous." Her mom took her into a warm embrace and then turned to the kids. "Kids, go into the living room. Nana and Papa will be there soon. I want to talk to your mom." She waited while the kids stomped off to the kitchen. They so hated to miss anything.

"Dana, I have something special for you." She rummaged in her gigantic purple purse. And rummaged. And rummaged.

Dana thought she heard the cawing of crows inside the purse.

"Mom, you ever thought of downsizing?" Valerie offered.

"A woman never downsizes a purse," her mother said. "You can put that on a T-shirt. Oh! Here it is!" She handed Dana a small blue box.

Dana gasped.

"They're *condoms*," her mother whispered…fiercely it seemed to Dana.

"Rubbers," her dad added, and then as if she was confused, "prophylactics. Used to use one all the time with your mother, back during the training days in the Guard. I had a supplier up in Big Rapids. He gave 'em to you in a brown paper bag, though if you walked out of his shop with a brown paper bag then everyone knew what you were getting anyway, so I never understood the point. Anyway. Now you can buy these anywhere. We got these…where?"

"Costco," her mother said. "I buy them in bulk. Hand them out as bingo prizes sometimes when we volunteer at the Lodge. You know, they don't just protect against pregnancy, but a whole host of…"

Dana had heard enough. She grabbed the box and stuffed it into her own purse.

"Great! Thanks!" she said hurriedly and then looked at Valerie. Val was no help at all. She just stood there, quivering with suppressed laughter.

"Okay, troops, let's start with some calisthenics!" her father boomed to the children. He reached over and touched the babies' toes. "You too, squirts. There's no 'I Can't' in the Guard. Ruby, Zach, come over here." The kids scrambled in from the kitchen and nearly ran into his legs. "Ten hut! We've got some serious exercising to do. Zach, you need to prepare to become a Jedi. And Ruby, a princess, above all else, needs to know a little self-defense." Her dad winked at Dana.

Dana just shook her head.

Chapter 36

Theodore finally emerged from the confines of Foodies. He felt pummeled. Angelique wasn't just a woman; she was a force. He'd trained her in less than ten minutes, if you could call giving her the code to things training. Fifteen minutes later she'd already reorganized the entire cashier's area and come up with an easier system for transactions. She worked with a force that virtually reverberated off her.

Mike and Theodore had watched from a distance, almost immediately brewing coffee and sitting down to give her space. It wasn't their idea to do so, but her order.

"Get out of my way, fellas," she said. "This place is a mess. You need structure. Efficiency. Just go sit somewhere until I tell you I'm ready for you."

After she'd reorganized everything, she motioned to them. "Look here," she said, pointing first to Mike with her red-fingernails and then to

Theodore. They both gulped. "Not only am I a retail whiz, I'm also a psychic. People pay me good money to tell their fortunes, but I'm going to give you a preview just for free. You," she said to Mike, "need to stop being a pussy. Man up a little bit and tell that woman what you feel. She will leave you high and dry unless you let her know that she's not just some sex goddess. And you," she said, pointing to Theodore, "you need to hold on. That's all I'm saying. Hold. On. And I'm not giving you any more advice than that. You won't hear me any way."

With that, she'd walked back to the closet, grabbed her coat and slipped it on. "I'm leaving. I'll be back tomorrow for a full day. I'm telling you now that things are going to be crazy, so you both better be prepared."

She left, a scent of cloves and cinnamon trailing after her.

"Did that seriously just happen?" Mike said. "I feel like she just walked out with my balls in her hand."

"And she's got mine in her pocket," Theodore agreed.

Now, driving to Coopersville, Theodore couldn't help but think, what had she meant by Hold On?

Chapter 37

Dana looked at her watch. In five minutes, if he was on time, she would be looking at her date. Correction. Not her date. Her business companion.

She scrunched her nose. Oh, forget it. Her date. She'd think of him as her date, even though he was strictly off limits. So in five minutes, she would be looking at her date. She wouldn't be the only one looking at him. There would also be her dad in fatigues, her mom wearing a I'm Over Sixty And Sexy sweatshirt, her sister Valerie, currently cradling both boys who were greedily sucking at her nipples, and Zach and Ruby, now sporting chocolate mustaches and beards thanks to the enormous chocolate turkeys—sort of like Easter candy—her mom had just given them.

Zach had chopped the head off the turkey first in an enormous bite and said "Look, Ruby. No blood. It's chocolate." Then Ruby had happily punched out the turkey's eyes and then went straight for its throat. It was disturbing.

This is my life, she chanted inwardly, still searching for that place of Zen that must exist somewhere with her. This is my life and he needs to see this or dating me is completely out of the question.

When they heard the car pull into the driveway, her father yelled, "Battle Stations!" Ruby screamed and hid in the closet. Zach grabbed his laser gun and pointed it at the door. Her dad stood next to Zach, hand on his shoulder, legs spread apart and back erect: a soldier's stance. Her mom detached one of the babies from Valerie, hung a blue spit cloth over her shoulder and began to pat his back. Valerie yelled, "Run upstairs! Run upstairs!"

Dana looked around frantically, not exactly sure what she was searching for. An exit? An emergency button to call the whole thing off? Because she wasn't sure what else to do, she listened to her sister. She ran upstairs. With all this running up and down the stairs, she wouldn't need to exercise for at least a week.

Chapter 38

Theodore thought he heard screaming, like four distinct voices screaming "Run!" and then something about an attack formation. He must be losing his mind. He adjusted his tie. The idea of wearing a shirt and tie and suit jacket seemed utterly ridiculous now. He should've gone for the I'm-a-dude-in-my-early-forties slacker mode and worn a Las Vegas T-shirt, but no. He'd wanted to appear professional. Like he had everything together. Like he wasn't suddenly as nervous as a teenager picking up his prom date. So, he'd opted instead for a shirt and tie, and jazzed it up by choosing a tie with Elvis's profile on it.

He reached for the doorbell, but before he could press it, the door swung open and Theodore stared straight into the upward-pointing muzzle of a gun held by a boy with brown war paint all over his face, and a tough looking grey-haired sergeant who said, "And just what are your intentions with my daughter?"

Chapter 39

The next part happened quickly. Dana heard the door open and her dad say that ridiculous remark. She heard Theodore say, "Uh…"

"Dad!" Dana called from the top of the stairs. "Don't do that!" Then she decided to end this silly charade. She'd run down, grab Theodore, kiss the kids on the head to avoid chocolate stains, and then they were out of here and fast. "I'm coming," she cried.

She ran down the stairs, forgetting that she was wearing a pair of ridiculously high—though super cute—red heels.

Later, in her mind she would replay just exactly how it happened. She'd run down the stairs a thousand times and never once slipped. How, then, with Theodore standing at the door, looking adorable in a suit with an Elvis tie, how did she actually slip down half the stairs? It must have been that moment before her foot landed on the action figure when she and Theodore had simply looked at each other. Then her heel had stepped on a trooper of some kind, she felt herself twist and she went flying.

It seemed to happen in slow motion. Valerie cried, "Noooooo!" Her mom turned to protect the babies from such a terrible view. Her dad scooped up Zach and lifted him out of the way. Theodore just stood there…which was why when she flipped over on the stairs and landed spread eagle on the ground at his feet, she was able to look right at him when he said, "Wow. That was quite the entrance." And then…"Hey. I like your shoes."

Chapter 40

To say total chaos erupted in the house was an understatement. First there was pure silence, and then the house quivered with a confused kind of laughter. The fall was so comedic, and it was magnified by the dazed look on Dana's face.

Theodore said, "Are you all right?"

Dana tried to say she was fine, but she couldn't breathe. She hoped her shoes were okay, but the shiny red heel of one of the shoes lay next to her head. Probably a sign that all was not well.

Zach bent to Dana, touched her hair, patted her cheek, and said, "Medic!"

Ruby said, "Mom. Mom. Mom. Ma? Mom. Mom. Mommy." But not in a panicked way, just in sort of a laid-back way. "Here's your shoe!" She swooped in and grabbed the heel.

Dana tried to say "thanks" but it came out more like a Frankenstein-like "mmmrrgg".

"Step aside! I had medical training in the Guard," her dad said.

Dana finally found her breath and said, "No. You. Don't." She took a deep breath, found her voice and said rather weakly, "Dad, you have no medical training whatsoever."

Her dad puffed out his chest, the look he wore when he was feeling cocky or falsely remembering his past. "I'll have you know I once sutured a wound using nothing but dental floss and a toothpick. That was back in '82, when I was doing a tour in Lansing."

"That tour was of the capital and not with the Guard at all," her mother said. "In fact, I was with you. We went on a Greyhound bus with forty other people." Her mom and dad continued to talk.

Dana was spread eagle on the floor, immobile, with a broken shoe and a bruised ego…and her parents were having the kind of conversation they'd have over a spaghetti dinner.

"Can you stand?" Theodore said and kneeled down. He smelled good. "Can I help you up?" He offered his hand. Dana took it. His hand was warm and strong and for the briefest flash, Dana imagined that hand running under her shirt and under the soft silk of her bra.

She sat up, shook her head, mostly to clear her mind of Theodore's hands over her skin. And attempted to stand. To anyone looking at her, they wouldn't even register that she was trying to stand because she was just sitting there. And sitting. Something wasn't right.

"Huh," she said. She should just be able to pop up from a seated position, shouldn't she? Hadn't she gotten off the floor a million times? The idea seemed overwhelming. Something was wrong with her foot. "Uhm…I think maybe…I think I maybe might have done something to my foot."

Valerie stepped in, released her son from her nipple and handed the baby to Theodore. Theodore held the baby like one might hold a baby alligator, as if afraid the baby would chomp his face off. She dropped to the ground and immediately took off what remained of Dana's red shoe. It seemed as if her foot had a bluish tint to it.

"You need to go to the ER," Valerie said calmly in the way that she would've said "You need to brush your teeth" as if it was something that, as her sister, she needed to share with her.

"That's ridiculous. I'm fine," Dana said. She tried to prove it by standing up. She gingerly pulled herself to her feet with Valerie's help, and then said, "See? I'm fine. No problem."

"You're only standing on one foot," Zach said.

"I can stand on one foot too," Ruby said. "Flamingos stand on one foot. Mom's a flamingo!"

Dana looked down. She was, indeed, standing on one foot, and the tears were starting to flow. The truth was, her foot was starting to swell, and she was feeling a wave of pain pulse through her. She'd envisioned a casual dinner with Theodore, her first real date in years. She'd thought of kissing him in the moonlight, and then coming home happy and content in the idea that she was a single mom and a woman and she could date and have something of her own. All of that evaporated.

Valerie grabbed the baby from Theodore. "All right, everyone. I'll take the babies in my car. Mom and Dad, you get the kiddos in yours. And Theodore…" He looked at her. "Nice to meet you. Would you mind holding on to Dana while I pull up the car? If you can help me load her in, we can get her to the ER."

Theodore blinked and said, "Hold on to her. Yes. Hold on. Yes! I can hold on!" And then looked around as if that meant something profound. "I mean, if it's all right with you, Dana, I'd be happy to take you to the

ER. It probably won't be that much fun for all the kids. I'll pull my car up and then between the two of us…" He looked at Valerie and then Dana's dad. "Between the three of us, we should be able to get her there." The group silently agreed. Theodore nodded and walked out the door to his car.

"I like him," Dana's mother said.

"Yeah, I like him too," her father agreed, somewhat regretfully.

"Is he married, Mom?" Zach asked. "Because you could marry him if you wanted."

Even with all the pain coursing through her, Dana smiled to herself. She wanted to say, "I already did." Instead, she said, "Well, a first date in an ER. That seems totally fitting somehow."

"It'll be great," Valerie said. "And if not great, at least it'll be memorable."

Chapter 41

Dana had one of those moments when you sort of float outside yourself and say *Hmm. Really? Really? This is really happening?* Even when she wrapped one arm around her dad and the other around Theodore, and they lifted her up and through the air to Theodore's car, even while that was actually happening she couldn't fully believe it truly was. If not for the ache in her foot and its swelling, she'd have sworn she was dreaming.

"Ouch!" she breathed when they set her in the car and she bumped her foot.

Her mom swept the men aside and repositioned Dana's legs in the car. She covered her with a crocheted blanket. "It's from the backseat of my car. We keep it there for emergencies. Although the only real emergency we've ever used it for was a quick roll in the hay on a very long road trip," she said with a smile. "Anyway. Be careful. Ask the doctors for drugs. They have really good ones at hospitals." Her mom patted her knee and then went back to the house.

It was useless to argue with her mother, so Dana simply tucked the blanket tighter around her legs. It actually felt comforting.

She looked out the car door to see Valerie standing in the doorway to her house holding her babies, and Zach and Ruby standing at her side, waving.

Her mom, of all things, was taking pictures. "It's still a date!" she called.

On that note, Dana struggled to get the door shut.

Theodore swept in, said, "Everything okay?" and when she nodded, he gently shut the door. She watched him shake her dad's hand and then sprint to the driver's side. Within moments he was belted in and they were pulling away from the curb.

"So on a scale of one to ten, how bad is the pain?" he asked her.

She didn't need to think about it. "About a nine point five."

"Glad it's not a ten, otherwise I'd take you straight to the ER. Since it's only a nine point five, do you want to pick up some food first?"

Dana smiled. "Oh, God," she said. "That would be wonderful. I'm absolutely starving, and we might have to wait a while in the ER."

"There's a burger joint on the way," Theo said. "It wasn't what I'd planned but, hey, there's something to be said for spontaneity." He turned and winked at her, and Dana had that curious body memory of his lips against hers, his tongue smoothing over hers.

"Burgers sound divine," she said, even though burgers were the furthest thing from her mind. She wasn't even thinking about the pain. She was thinking about when there might be a moment when she could kiss him again, and hoped it would be before they x-rayed her.

Chapter 42

Throughout the whole ER ordeal, Theodore just repeated to himself two simple words "hold on". He just needed to Hold On. Damned if Angelique hadn't been right. He pulled up to the doors of the ER, and an orderly came out, took one look at Dana's ever increasingly swelling foot and raced back for a wheelchair. Once Dana was transferred from the car to the wheelchair and Theodore parked, he held on to the chair's handles and pushed, trying not to bash her foot against the narrow corridors.

"I feel so ridiculous," Dana said, leg extended out straight in front of her.

"You'll only be ridiculous if they can't figure out a way to make your leg lay flat again."

Dana smiled. In the waiting room, they made small talk as Dana filled out the paperwork. Theodore held her purse. "You doing okay?" he asked her and she nodded. There were just two people in front of them. One was a hefty guy who looked like he might've been the original Paul Bunyan, 100 years ago. He was old and massive. They could hear the nurse speaking loudly to him. "Mr. Everett, your blood sugar is dangerously high. Do you remember that you're a diabetic?"

"What's that?" he asked just as loudly back.

"You. Are. Diabetic. What did you eat tonight?"

"I ate what I always eat. French fries, fried chicken, and some chocolate cake."

They watched the nurse wheel him away, repeating to him that he had to control his diet.

The other patient was moaning in the corner.

Theodore leaned over to Dana and whispered into her ear. "See? It could be worse. Worst case scenario you sprained your ankle or something. At least you're not a diabetic lumberjack. Or that lady in the corner. She must have a serious case of stomach flu."

Dana snickered. "Theo, the woman is in labor. Her stomach flu is called having a baby."

Theodore sat back and stared at the woman for a moment. "Ah. That explains all the moaning then."

Finally, the nurse called them into the back room. "Dana Kupiac!"

Theodore pushed her forward.

"Are you the husband?" the nurse asked him.

Theodore didn't know what to say. He was holding Dana's purse and the wheelchair's handles, and he didn't want to let go. He didn't want Dana to have to go through whatever she was about to go through on her own. He thought briefly of Las Vegas and was about to say something when Dana said, "Yep. He sure is." Then she said conspiratorially, "Well, in some cultures you are. What happened in Vegas…"

He nodded. Surprisingly, pretending to be Dana's husband was a lot of fun.

Chapter 43

The appointment took about an hour. The nurse asked a lot of very personal questions of Dana, and Theodore learned all sorts of things, stuff that one usually didn't get to know until the third, fourth, maybe one-hundredth date. She wasn't allergic to anything, she'd had her period two weeks ago, she'd never broken a bone before, there was no cancer in her family, she was not currently pregnant.

After the deluge of questions, Dana added, "And I like long walks on the beach," to which Theodore tried not to laugh.

"Oh, I don't think you'll be walking anytime soon," the nurse said, then patted her knee. "Don't worry though. This will just give your husband the opportunity to take extra good care of you over the holidays. Maybe he'll even have to bake the turkey."

As soon as the nurse left, Dana looked down in her lap, and Theodore saw that she was crying. He held her hand and waited.

"I think it's broken," she said. "I mean when I went flying in the air and then landed, I felt my foot do something, like it rolled in a way I've never felt before and now…now…" The tears were coming heavy now.

Theodore let go of her hand, grabbed a box of tissue, and dabbed at her eyes. Then he held her hand again and sat across from her.

"And now?" he prompted.

"I'm in a lot of pain. I don't think I can joke around or be funny or relaxed or charming. I'm sorry. I'm sorry if this is the worst date you've ever had. And, oh, I didn't mean to say this is a date. It's business. Just business, and I'm really sorry but I can't even think about business right now, and I know you want to just get home as quickly as possible or maybe call up that fiancée of yours. And…I just…what am I going to do?"

Theodore just looked at her. Her makeup was running down her cheeks and her eyes were red and puffy. Her foot was stretched out and turning an alarming shade of purple. "You just hold on," he said. "This probably isn't the best time to say this, Dana, but," he lifted her chin so she could look him in the eyes, "I don't have a fiancée anymore."

She didn't seem to understand. "What? Where is she?"

"We broke up. I broke it up. I ended it. It's over. It's a good thing. It's complicated. It's just that you…me…my life…" He shrugged his shoulders. He couldn't seem to put any of it into words, so he did the best thing he could think of.

He leaned forward and kissed her, gently.

Chapter 44

"What you have here," said the doctor, a petite woman with a no-nonsense kind of attitude, "is called a Jones Fracture. See this line on your x-ray?" The doctor pointed and both Dana and Theodore nodded. "Good news is, it'll heal. Bad news is, you'll need a cast for a month and then a walking cast for another month, and then we'll see."

Dana was trying to process everything. "Two months and then you'll see?"

The doctor nodded. "It's unfortunately a bone that takes a long time to heal. It happens to be in a part of the foot that just doesn't get a lot of blood flow. It'll take two months at minimum, possibly closer to three."

"Oh," she said. It was all she could manage.

"And we'll have to send you to a foot specialist to get casted. You'll need to wait until the swelling goes down. It might take a week for that to happen. Until then, you need to keep your foot elevated. You the husband?"

Theodore nodded. It was more a reaction than anything. Once he nodded, it seemed silly to take it back.

The doctor continued, "Put her on the couch. Make sure she rests. Do you have kids?"

"Two," Dana said.

"Well, your husband is going to have to be dad *and* mom for a while. Keep movement to a minimum. Take pain medication as needed. Prop pillows on the couch and get the foot above your heart. Use frozen peas to help with the swelling. And as for sex…"

"Uh," both Dana and Theodore said.

The doctor plowed forward. "If she's willing and you have a copy of the kama sutra or you're really creative, you might be able to make it work."

The doctor smiled and then left.

Dana didn't know what to say. Theodore started laughing. "It's not funny!" she said and slapped his arm.

"It is kind of funny," he said.

"Yeah, well, shit." Dana could barely speak. How was she going to get through the next two months in a cast, on crutches, taking care of two kids and a small business and teaching and, oh God, the holidays… "Thanksgiving!" she cried. "It's at my house. And my jams and…"

She was about to start crying again when Theodore said, "You don't have to do everything alone, Dana. You've got a great family who will help you, and if you'll let me, I'd like to help you too. I know it's weird and maybe pretty quick, but I make a mean turkey. A turkey so mean it could bite you back. I could, you know, come over. On Thanksgiving. And before. Whatever. Whatever you want. And after the Foodies' opening ceremony, I've got a lot more free time." He didn't mention that after the cancelled wedding, he'd also have more time. He didn't need to.

"You want to spend Thanksgiving with me? And my kids? And my crazy family?" Dana could hardly believe it. "And you want to cook?"

"If you'll let me," he said.

Dana could see it all happening. She really could. She could see him coming over, rolling up his shirtsleeves, putting on an apron and getting to work. She could see him joking with her kids, getting them to help him make a pie, all while she rested in the living room. Yes, it was a fantasy, but at the same time it seemed entirely possible, and it scared her to death. The tears really started flowing then, the way water rushes during a flood. She just cried and cried and cried.

"Did I say something wrong?" Theodore asked.

She shook her head. "You said something right," she said. "I just… Right now, I just need to get home and go to sleep. But I don't even know how I'm going to get up the stairs." Her head was full. Her heart was full. She was in pain and scared and right now she wished that this was a date and she was ready for a relationship and he hadn't just broken a promise to someone. Right now, she wished that she'd been the one he'd promised something to. Somehow, it sort of felt like she was. He'd promised to help her. To be there for her, even if only for a short time. Could she trust that?

Theodore reached over and put his hand on her knee. "That doesn't hurt, does it?"

"No. My knee is okay."

"Okay, good. We'll figure it out, Dana," he said softly. "I mean it."

Somehow, she believed him.

Chapter 45

It was late at night when Mike finally made it up the steep hill to his apartment. He'd tried everything he could to talk himself out of what he was about to do. He'd cleaned Foodies until it sparkled. He went for a five-mile run. He drove to East Grand Rapids and had a gigantic dinner for one at Olives, in the hopes of eating himself into a delightful food coma. Nothing helped.

Who was he kidding? Nothing could help. There wasn't a cure for his kind of malady. When he looked back on his life, he looked back on it with a sense of shame. He'd had three women say "I Do" to him, and he'd never taken any of them seriously. He'd broken hearts and his own bank account. He'd started over more times than he could count. He'd misused love and affection. He'd been a grade A asshole. So what made him think he deserved a woman like Mavis?

He didn't. And he knew he could no longer resist trying.

He was exhausted. He couldn't fight it anymore. His plan was to knock on her door, tell her he loved her, grovel at her feet, plead with her to share her life with him. He'd promise her anything. He'd mean it. He wouldn't cheat. He wouldn't abandon. A man could change. He'd been beaten down enough by life and his own choices. He was ready to become someone new.

He had his monologue all worked out, only he never got the chance to use it. Mavis was waiting for him. She opened the door, grabbed his hand, and without a word led him upstairs into her apartment.

In the morning, they'd put a For Rent sign in his downstairs apartment.

It didn't matter that they hadn't known each other long or that there was such an age difference. It didn't matter that she was too good for him or that he'd been a cheat in his previous relationships. When they were together, everything else slipped away. It was just Mike and Mavis and a quiet understanding between them. A gentle love that he'd never experienced before. He didn't feel like he was rushing into anything at all. Instead, he felt like he'd finally come home.

Chapter 46

It was just hours until the opening of Foodies. They were ready. Angelique was dressed in a hot pink wool dress, Mike looked presentable in a suit and tie, and Theodore was wearing the same clothes he'd fallen asleep in last night, complete with Elvis tie, although admittedly, Elvis looked a little tired.

When Theodore had rushed to the store in the morning, Mike took one look at him and said, "Man, you got lucky!" and he didn't see the point in correcting him. Part of him had felt lucky, strangely enough. He and Dana's sister Valerie helped Dana to the couch and balanced her foot on a tower of pillows. Theodore then helped Valerie load the twins and endless baby supplies into her minivan. Dana's parents took Zach and Ruby to their condo to spend the night.

Theodore sat in a small reading chair and watched until Dana had finally dropped off to sleep. He fell asleep in the chair, head drooped forward, so that by morning he had a killer crick in his neck. Sometime in the middle of the night he thought he heard her mentioning something about The E and Las Vegas and I do, I do, I do, but he chalked it up to the Vicodin she was on.

In the morning he was awakened by the sounds of Dana's kids running up the walkway screaming, "Mom! Mommy!" The door flew open and there was the chaos of kids and grandparents and kisses and more pills for Dana and a fresh bag of peas for her foot.

He tried to smooth his hair down, caught Dana's eye and lifted his hand in a goodbye. He wanted to do more, but didn't know what. Kiss her? Take care of her? Stay with her? Yes. He wanted to do that. But you didn't do that on the first date, even if in another life—somewhere in a parallel universe called Las Vegas—you were actually married to the woman. So he'd simply waved and said goodbye.

Looking at the time of 9:30 AM, he knew he needed to get to Foodies as quickly as possible, so he'd driven straight there, thinking he'd clean up in the bathroom and look as good as new. He'd been wrong. His hair refused to obey him and displayed an errant personality with tufts sticking up here and there.

"Handsome," Angelique said. "I'd say you looked like you made love last night, but you're missing that afterglow look. Mostly, you just look worn out. Did you take my advice and hold on?"

"I did," Theodore agreed.

"Good. That's a step in the right direction."

That was the end of the small talk because, like it or not, Foodies was open. Angelique, Mike and Theodore went to the door.

"Okay," Mike said. "Here goes everything." He unlocked the door. Angelique turned on the neon sign that said OPEN and then…they waited. Really. They stood lined up in the front of the store, all three of them, waiting.

"That's sort of anti-climactic," Theodore said after a few minutes.

Angelique walked behind the deli to grind some coffee beans. "Oh, they're coming all right. Probably not until after noon. But we better get ready."

An hour later, they had their first customer—a petite blonde woman who looked like she had at one time been a cheerleader. She probably was still a cheerleader, even though she looked like she was in her forties. She walked in, asked Angelique for a coffee.

Angelique brewed her one, handed it to her, then leaned over and kissed her. Theodore heard Mike gasp. Or was that his own gasp? Was Angelique going to treat every customer this way?

"Oh, stop looking so shocked," she said as if in response. "This is my wife," she said. "Don't let her perkiness confuse you. She'll kill you with a stray thought."

"Oh, pish-shaw. I'm Rachel and Angelique is just messing with you," she said. "I won't kill you with a stray thought, because I never have stray thoughts. I could kill you with a pencil though, if you're not nice to my woman."

Mike said, "Uh…"

The response seemed good enough for Rachel. She paid for the coffee, said her good-byes and good-lucks, and then was out of the store.

After that, Theodore didn't notice who came in…but there was a steady stream. They'd put out a lunch special for the deli, and college students and business people strolled in. They looked at the wine, the chips, the gourmet dips and spreads, and they started buying.

The day raced by in a swirl of stocking and restocking, the sounds of the cash register keys clicking, and Angelique calling out for help behind the deli. It was absolutely magical. Theodore lost himself in it. This was what he'd been born for. Not just owning a business but also talking to people, connecting, and he realized that this sudden new life, one without Sarah peering over his shoulder and criticizing his every move, this new life had the potential to be wonderful.

Amidst the noise and the laughter and later the clicks of the Grand Rapids Press's reporter's camera, Theodore thought about Dana. He wished, somehow, she could see this. She wished she could see that among their top sellers of the day was her Raspberry Ripple Jam, perfect for toast or as a filling between double chocolate cake.

He looked at his watch. In a few days, he'd be able to tell her just how successful she was. He could barely wait until Thanksgiving.

While helping a customer carry twelve bottles of wine to her car, he thought, again, how peculiar life was and how quickly everything could change…sometimes for the better.

Chapter 47

Dana thought about how quickly everything in life could change. A week ago, she was just starting her business and rushing from work to daycare to home and spending every waking moment taking care of either her kids or her job. Now, she was flat on her back on the couch, leg balanced precariously on a stack of six pillows, watching *Beaches* and crying her eyes out.

Her mom handed her some tissue. "Oh, this movie just about kills me," her mom said, sniffling. "I hate it and love it equally."

"I know," Dana said. "It's just so…beautiful." She felt her own tears building and waved the tissue in the air. She was having a major estrogen moment, but decided not to fight it. "Their friendship. So beautiful, you know?" Her voice came out in an emotional croak. "How when Barbara Hershey gets cancer and then Bette Midler decides to raise her child and you can totally tell she doesn't know what to do, and she has to do it all on her own, and then Barbara dies! She dies! And the little girl and Bette are there together but you can see there's a real bond there…and it's like…" Dana paused, feeling like she was on the verge of a great epiphany. "And it's like their friendship will just go…on…you know? But through the daughter?" She blew her nose…for quite a while.

Her mother sat quietly for a moment. "You're either PMS'ing or in love," she finally said.

Dana laughed. She *was* awfully emotional, but she didn't think she could chalk it up to just PMS'ing or love. And the whole idea of love just sent her further down the path of an emotional breakdown. It had been a long time since she'd felt love, and now she was developing a severe crush on a man she'd had a fling with in Las Vegas, who turned out to be engaged, who turned out to dump his fiancée just like that. Bam! Why couldn't she meet and fall for someone dependable. Like a car salesman.

A weird garble sound emitted from her throat. More sobs.

She'd already been crying most of the day, and not really for any reason. Sure, her foot hurt, but with the pain medication it was at a dull ache. She wasn't crying about that, nor was she crying about *Beaches*. She wasn't even crying about the absurdity of having a broken foot. She was crying about *everything*. Everything that had happened from the moment that Paul told her he didn't love her. Maybe she was even crying for the years before that happened, when neither of them said the words, but knew it to be true anyway.

"Mom, I think…" She paused, wondering if she should say anything. It was hard to speak. Her throat was tight, clenched with the kind of pain that only swallowed sorrow caused.

"Spill it, kiddo," her mom said. "I've been trying to get you to talk for months, and now's the time. You've got to get the words out or you'll never stop crying."

Dana nodded. It was true. She took a deep breath and then spilled it. All of it. Everything she could think of. It was actually surprisingly easy to put her emotions into a sentence.

"Paul left me. He left me. But it's more than that. He left our family and now he…he's starting over. It's so easy for him. He gets to start over. Did you know their baby is due any time? He cancelled the last two weekends with the kids, and I just can't… It's like there's this hole in my heart where he's concerned. And it's sad too because it isn't even about me. It's about the kids…and…I'm lonely." She took a breath, looked at her mom, but her mom said nothing. It was silent encouragement to go on.

"And I'm really lonely. And tired. I've been doing so much, all on my own. And, yes, I have you and dad and Valerie and Vick but it's not the same. Every time the kids need me, I'm there. Every bill that comes in, I pay. Every moment I'm working, trying to earn money. There's no time for me. There's no time for hope. There's no time to date. And I finally met a man who…and he…" She couldn't say the words. He was unreliable. Clearly. And maybe he just wanted a fling again, only this time, one that was consummated. And dammit, part of her wanted that too.

"It's like this whole year I've been moving so fast that I haven't had a chance to breathe let alone feel anything and now I just feel…" She started crying again. "I just feel *everything*."

Her mom reached over and started smoothing her hair. As a child, Dana had loved it when her mom played with her hair, and it was still one of her favorite things. Her mom was quiet for a time, making sure that Dana had had her say. Dana felt relief as the words left her.

"Of course you feel everything," her mom said. "It makes sense. You've been moving so fast you've been outrunning your emotions. I'm not kidding. You really have. And now, life has told you to take a break.

It's probably told you a few times, but you weren't listening, so now life has broken your foot. It's forcing you to slow down. To ask for help. To let the people who love you, help you. Now, life is telling you to stop for a bit. Take some time. You cancelled your classes, you can't cook, you can't run after the kids. Nope. You've got to just sit here and feel it. So feel it. And let it out."

That started a whole new onslaught of tears, but this time Dana didn't fight it. She let the tears wash over and through her. She'd worked so hard this year to pay the mortgage, get back into the career world. She'd fought for everything to stay afloat. She'd mourned the breakup of her marriage as well as the understanding that it was for the best. She'd felt certain that her life as a woman, a woman capable of sharing passion was over, and now she'd met someone she had a peculiar connection with. She didn't want to trust him, and couldn't fight the temptation to try with him anyway. To hope that he was interested in her, even if only for a short time. And now, flat on her back, it seemed that running was no longer an option.

When the tears finally subsided, Dana said, "Mom, this Theo…"

"Yes."

"I met him before. In Las Vegas. We spent two crazy days together. We laughed, we ate out, we saw shows and on the last night…"

"Did you use a condom?" her mother asked gently.

"Mom! What is it with you and condoms! No! I didn't!"

"Dana, you cannot take that risk. You need to protect yourself in more ways than one. There is a steady rise of sexually transmitted diseases and I know…"

Dana took a deep breath. "Mom. No. Stop. We didn't need to use a condom because we didn't sleep together. We just…kissed. And we got married in a chapel. But we just kissed."

Her mother didn't say anything to that.

"Mom?" Dana asked.

"Still processing," she said and then after a moment, "You got married in Vegas and didn't call us? We would've flown out there!"

Dana laughed to herself. Most moms would've chastised their daughter for being so spontaneous and foolish. Her mom, instead, was upset because she hadn't been invited. "No, it wasn't like that. We didn't fill out a marriage license. We didn't sign anything. It was just a joke."

"Hmmm," her mom said. "It's interesting," she said finally.

"What?"

"All of it. That you'd meet him in Vegas and you pretended to marry him, and then he showed up here and…yes. Seems perfectly clear to me."

"What does?"

"Las Vegas was just a rehearsal. You're gearing up for the real thing…but this time…please invite your father and me. I have a silver dress I've been dying to wear. It's very low-cut. It may even give your father a heart attack, but if it kills him? Well. What a way to go."

"Mom! I'm not talking about marrying him. It's complicated. While we were in Vegas, while we were having our 'time' together, he was engaged. And now he just broke up with her. How dependable is that?"

Her mother thought about it. "You're saying he met you in Vegas, you had fun, but didn't cross any lines physically, he met you again here, and soon after he broke up with his fiancée, and then came to take you to dinner, but only after he'd terminated his engagement."

Hearing her mom say it like that made Dana pause. It didn't sound as dastardly as she'd though.

"Is it possible, Dana, that this Theodore is honorable? Is it possible that he thought he was happy and then when he met you, he had a hint of what happiness could be? If he wasn't happy with her, should he have married her, or is it more honorable to end the wrong relationship in pursuit of the right one? And by the right one, I mean, in pursuit of you?

"I know as your mother I should tell you to be cautious, but as your friend, I can tell you that when something is right, it's easy. And why deny the truth of that? Sometimes you just *know*." She squeezed Dana's hand and smiled. "You're running, my sweet girl. You've been running most of your life. Maybe life is telling you to slow down. Maybe it's time you let someone catch you. Maybe life broke your foot just to help you out." With that, her mother got up to get them fresh coffee from the kitchen.

Dana blew her nose yet again. At this rate she'd need to stock up on bulk boxes of tissue. There was no point in telling her mother she was crazy, that Las Vegas wasn't a rehearsal at all, that she and Theodore just met and to say that they belonged together somehow was ridiculous. There was no point in arguing any of those things because, the truth was, Dana felt sure that he *was* The One. Falling down at his feet was just the universe's way of telling Dana to stop fighting it and to stop running, and she certainly wasn't running now. She would be very easy to catch, if he decided to chase after her.

Chapter 48

At seven o'clock, after the press had interviewed them and taken pictures, after they'd sold all their sandwiches, after Angelique had counted down the till, they finally turned off the sign and bolted the lock.

"Wow," Mike said, leaning against the door.

"Wow," Theodore echoed.

"Mother fucker," Angelique said, to which they both nodded. It really was the only phrase that captured the pure sentiment of the moment.

"That was a good day," Mike said. "A really good day. And I am so tired I just want to go home and sleep."

"I don't think *today* has anything to do with why you need to sleep," Angelique said. "What's your lady friend's name?"

"What lady friend?" Mike said, actually looking around the room to make sure she was talking to him.

"The lady friend you're so enamored with that you can't keep your hands off her."

"Oh. That friend." Mike cleared his throat. "Don't laugh. Her name is Mavis."

Theodore felt his eyes widen. Mavis sounded like a very old-fashioned kind of name.

"There's a slight age difference, okay? But I don't even see it. And she's…well, goddammit, don't look at me that way. She's unbelievable. Sexy. Smart. Funny. Goddammit! Why can't a man date an older woman if he wants to? Women date older men all the time and no one says a thing. It's not like she's a grandmother or anything. I mean, okay, yes, she has grandchildren but…Annette Bening is in her fifties."

Theodore and Angelique didn't say a word.

"And, yes, I'm fucking in love with her. I love her. Not Annette Bening. I'm not talking about her. I love Mavis! Okay? Huh? Are you happy? Are you satisfied?"

"I think the question is are *you* satisfied?" Angelique said as she pulled on her coat.

"Yes, I'm fucking satisfied! I've never been happier in all my life!" Mike bellowed. The words reverberated. The three of them looked at each other for a moment. Mike blinked, adjusted his tie and said softly, "Okay, then. Mavis and I have dinner plans. I will see you two tomorrow."

Angelique and Theodore watched Mike grab his coat and rush out of the store. Once he was gone, they both broke out into quiet laughter.

"He's got it bad," Theodore said. "I haven't seen him act this way in…well…since the last time he got married."

"He's going to marry this one too," Angelique said. "Mark my words. And you…"

Theodore cut her off. “Don’t tell me my future, Angelique. Let it be a surprise.”

She smiled at him. “Then if it’s going to be a surprise, you best get a move on. You have another date, don’t you?”

“Yes,” he said. “I do.”

Chapter 49

There are times in life when you think you know exactly what is about to happen. This had happened to Theodore countless times with Sarah. He could envision entire conversations with her.

"I made a goat cheese ravioli for dinner tonight," he'd say. "You want to join me?"

"I'm not eating something that says baaaaaaa," Sarah would respond.

"Actually, I think that's more of a sheep."

"Whatever. I'm not eating something from a goat. You know this, Theodore. Plus, I'm dieting for the wedding. Just give me some lettuce. But not the fancy schmancy lettuce that you put in stuff. I want good old-fashioned lettuce. Iceberg. I want iceberg."

Theodore had actually envisioned this conversation once on his way home and pulled off to stop at a grocery store to pick up some plain lettuce. And everything that evening had gone according to how he'd thought. She didn't want his food, she made fun of him, she talked about the wedding, he tried to slip away in his mind. And now he really had slipped away…from her. It was amazing that you could be engaged to someone one moment, and free the next.

With Dana, however, he had yet to get any envisioning right. From the moment he met her, she'd been a constant surprise. He just couldn't predict what she was going to do next. From the experience in Vegas, to her dropping off jams, to kissing her in a darkened restaurant, to their first official date with both of them eating hamburgers as quickly as possible before heading into the ER…to now…pulling up to her house. He didn't know what to expect. What was beyond those doors waiting for him? He was both terrified and intrigued.

With Dana Kupiac, it seemed anything was possible.

Chapter 50

Dana heard the car pull up and called out, "Kiddos, Theo is here! Can you get the door?"

"Sure!" they screamed; then she heard them running to the door.

Sometimes she felt like her children were puppies, the way that they ran everywhere and fell over each other. She tried to prop herself up on the couch a little and adjusted the bag of peas on her foot. A few hours ago her sister had taken over Sick Duty from her mom, and she'd helped Dana put makeup on.

"Your eyes are totally puffy," Valerie had said.

"Well, I had a bit of a crying jag."

"Really? How little?"

"About two hours."

"Nice one. Good job. Let me get the waterproof mascara in case you feel like you're going to start up again."

Dana had said she didn't think there were any tears left in her, she'd cried so hard.

They'd done her hair and a light makeup, and she felt relatively normal again. Her foot, however, was wrapped in gauze and a bandage. They'd taken it off to check the swelling and had marveled at the swirls of blue and purple.

"It's like a rainbow," Ruby had breathed.

Tomorrow, hopefully the swelling would subside enough and Dana could get a cast on it and then—fingers crossed—be mobile again. As it was, she could use her crutches to get back and forth from the bathroom, but she'd already banged her foot on the table once and was fearful of anything touching it.

After changing into clean clothes, with a little help from Valerie, she'd convinced her sister to head home and take care of her own family. Vick was minding the babies and had called to say they were trying to nurse on him.

"Will they ever stop?" Valerie cried. "I mean, my nipples are so popular with those two I feel like a cow. And now all I seem to talk about is nipples. Jesus. When am I going to have a normal life again?"

Dana looked at her kids. Zach had his Clone Wars helmet on and was repeatedly running into a wall while Ruby was trying to feed her Elnono a snack by shoving a sandwich into the poor stuffed elephant's face. "I hate to tell you, sis, that while your time as a cow might end, you will never, ever be normal again. Go home. Be with your babies. I include Vick in that."

"I don't want to leave you alone just yet," Valerie had said.

"Don't worry. Theodore is coming over in a couple of hours, the kids are fed, and they can help out if I need anything. Right kids?" she called. "Can you help me out if Aunt Val goes home?"

Both Ruby and Zach said, "No!"

"See? I'll be fine."

Valerie had reluctantly agreed. Before leaving she asked the kids a thousand questions: *Do you need food, need to go to the bathroom, do you need anything from upstairs.* Then turned and asked Dana the exact same things.

"We're fine!" Dana said. "Go home!"

Finally, Valerie had.

As soon as she left, the kids started crying about wanting a snack. Dana tried to get on her crutches and managed to get to the kitchen, then realized she couldn't open the refrigerator because she was holding onto her crutches. Then she realized that if she got the refrigerator open, she wouldn't be able to carry anything to the counter. Her foot was already throbbing. She could maybe manage things by hopping on one foot instead of using crutches and carrying things, if the food was encased in plastic wrap. Then again, just the idea of jumping around was terrifying. What if she slipped and fell again? If even *walking* with the crutches hurt like mad, what would hopping around feel like? She needed a real cast and one of those carts to wheel around on, and she didn't have either.

"Tell you what," she'd said to Ruby and Zach. "Why don't you guys fix yourself a snack and have a picnic in the living room?" The kids had cheered and Dana awkwardly used her crutches to clunk back to the living room and fall onto the couch.

The snack had consisted of grapes, cheese, chocolate cake, juice boxes, chips, and ham…basically whatever the kids could get out of the refrigerator or pull from the cupboard. And the food was everywhere. On the floor, on the reading chair, in the kitchen. All Dana could do was shake her head. Finally, when the doorbell rang, she felt a flutter of relief. The two hours alone with her kids had been more stressful than she'd realized. If they had fallen or needed help, she would not have been able to help them.

Zach swung open the door.

"Hey there," Theodore said. "Remember me?"

"Actually, I do," Zach said, seeming much older than six. "You're Theo."

"That's right. Is your mom here? May I come in?"

"That depends," Dana heard Zach say. "Are you married?"

Dana felt herself cringe and almost cried, "Zach, get away from the door!" but she didn't have time. Theodore took the question seriously.

"I am not married," he said soberly.

"Well, you can marry my mom if you want. She doesn't have anyone. Course, you'd have to ask her, and she would have to *want* to marry you, and you'd have to be really nice to me and Ruby and probably give us stuff, and you'd have to move in here because this is our house and we like it and… Do you play light sabers?"

"I do indeed."

"Okay, then," Zach conceded. "You can come in. But remember what I said about my mom. She's on the couch. Don't touch her foot."

Dana stifled a laugh. See? Her life was never normal, and she was very happy with that.

Chapter 51

When Theo came into the living room, led by Zach and Ruby, he first took a look at all the food everywhere and then looked at Dana on the couch. Even with her foot in the air, her toes sticking out, she looked beautiful.

She wasn't beautiful in the way that magazines told you a woman should be beautiful. She wasn't skinny and her skin wasn't stretched. She was natural. She was beautiful in a quiet way. A gentle way. A way that was real and honest and simple. Her brown hair was pulled into a ponytail, and her eyes sparkled with laughter. It was one of the things he loved about her, how she could be broken and have something awful happen, and her eyes still sparkled with humor.

He took a deep breath. In his mind, he'd really had the thought that her humor was "just one of the things I love about her". Love? What? That wasn't possible. He barely knew the woman! And he'd just broken up with the woman he'd been engaged to. Had planned on marrying, had said over and over, "I love you, too". With Sarah, though, he'd never had that sort of moment where he thought "this is one of the things I love about her". Somehow, inexplicably, Dana felt like the missing puzzle piece to his life, a piece he didn't even know he had been missing until she came in and filled it.

He shook the thoughts away and crossed over and kissed her forehead. "Mind if I pick this stuff up?" he said. "Looks like the kids had a feast."

"I know. I know. I should've stopped it, but sometimes you just have to let go and let life happen."

He nodded. He bent to pick up some smooshed cake and then suddenly was tackled from behind.

Ruby leapt onto his back and cried, "Horsey ride!"

Zach said, "He can't give you a horsey ride, Ruby. He's cleaning up."

"Maybe I can do both," Theodore said. "Tell you what, I'll give you one horsey ride, and then you guys help me clean up, and then maybe I have something for you in my car."

The kids seemed to consider this. "What kind of something?" asked Zach.

"It's a surprise," Theodore said.

Ruby jumped off his back and immediately grabbed a cup of applesauce and marched it directly to the kitchen. In a few minutes, the entire living room was spotless, and the kids were jumping up and down for the surprise.

Theodore went to his car and grabbed the two little gifts. They were something he'd picked up after leaving Foodies. There was a convenience store a few stores down from his, and he'd found the motorized gerbils.

One was pink and the other was black. When you pushed a button, the gerbils laughed and giggled and spun in circles.

Zach snatched his and said "Awesome! Let's have a race!"

Ruby reluctantly agreed, but only after she'd given her gerbil a haircut.

Finally, Theodore grabbed a chair and pulled it close to the couch. "Can I get you anything?" he asked.

Dana pointed to her lips. He leaned over and kissed her gently.

"How about right here?" she pointed to her eyebrow. He kissed there too. "And here?" She turned her head, exposing the soft, delicate curve of her neck. He kissed there too, once, twice, a handful of times.

"Mmm. Nice," she said. "Thanks for coming over."

"My pleasure. Really."

"I want to talk about you and hear all about your day, but I have a confession to make," Dana said. "I'm starving. I have some spanakopita in the freezer. Actually, it's a pie. Can you put it in the oven? We could have a nice dinner of spanakopita and salad and pears and…I don't know whatever else is in there."

Theodore didn't know what to say. "You made spanakopita?"

"Well, before I broke my foot, yeah. And then I froze it."

"But that's with feta, right? With goat cheese?" Theodore held his breath.

"Tons of it. And spinach too, so you feel like you're eating something healthy, even though it's probably awful for you. But good awful. It's even topped with crisp phyllo."

Theodore beamed. He couldn't believe his luck.

Chapter 52

With the help of Zach and Ruby, Theodore cooked the spanakopita. *Cooked* was pushing it. He put it in the oven and pressed 350 and then start. But he did make the salad. Mixed greens—no iceberg—with sliced pear, and he found walnuts in the cupboard and toasted them and made a balsamic vinegar dressing. Dana had said to him to make whatever he wanted using whatever was on hand.

In most households, this would mean ranch dressing and frozen pizza. But Dana's cupboards held something far more surprising: world spices and gourmet ingredients. She had pancetta in the refrigerator, all the spices one could wish for to make homemade curry; she had lentils and beans and organic chicken breasts. There were lemons and capers, and Theodore knew that if he wanted to make chicken piccata for her, he could.

In fact, he did.

Zach and Ruby pushed up two chairs from the dining room to the counter, and Theodore gave them each a chicken breast wrapped in plastic wrap.

"All right, troops," he began seriously. "I want you to pound this chicken flat. As flat as you can, but you don't want to break it. You got that?"

"We hit the chicken?" Ruby asked. "Like with our hands?"

"Oh, no. Good cooking is about using tools." He gave them each a meat tenderizer. They were heavy, so Ruby had a hard time holding onto it and then WHACK! She got the hang of it.

"Sweet!" Zach said. And then he went crazy on the chicken breast.

"What is going on in there?" Dana called from the couch. Then after a pause, where Theodore was certain she was sniffing, she said, "Whatever it is, keep at it."

Once the breasts were flattened, Ruby helped squeeze the lemon for fresh juice. Theodore found plastic gloves for Zach and put him in charge of tossing the chicken in flour. Then as the spanakopita warmed and turned golden in the oven, Theodore quickly cooked the chicken and made the lemon caper sauce with a little butter and deglazed the pan with wine. The house smelled warm and citrusy and delicious.

"What about dessert?" Ruby said.

Theodore checked the cupboards. He wanted to use one of Dana's jams or sauces, not just to suck up to her, although that wouldn't hurt, but also because her stuff was damn good. Checking the refrigerator, he found whipping cream, and in the pantry was a selection of high quality chocolate.

"I don't know about you guys, but I'm thinking chocolate mousse with a little touch of your mom's Raspberry Ripple."

Zach said, "Dude. Seriously. You can marry my mom if you want."

"Do you want to do that?" Ruby asked sincerely. She looked up at him and her deep blue eyes sparkled like the blue of a perfectly cloudless sky.

Theodore quietly answered, "If your mom will have me, kiddos. I just might."

Chapter 53

Dana insisted on moving to the dining room for dinner, but first she'd have to get up from the couch. "With food smelling that good, it would be a shame to eat it on a TV tray. No. I want to eat like a regular…" She was about to say *family* but stopped herself.

"Like a regular person," she finished. As much as she loved having Theodore here, and she felt attracted to him and wanted to spend as much time as she could with him getting to know all about him and why he was so serious but wore Elvis ties, and what made them click so quickly…she was also scared. She wasn't sure what was happening, although whatever it was, it felt natural. That scared her most of all.

She should've waited to introduce the kids to him. She really hadn't even intended to. It had sort of just happened. She heard of other single moms having passionate affairs with men and keeping their home life entirely separate. The trouble was, Dana didn't want to lead two lives. She didn't want to be a woman in one, and a mom in the other. And it also wasn't an option to date someone unless they were good with her kids. She still didn't even know if she *should* date him, although after talking to her mom, Dana was beginning to suspect that maybe she should.

Even though it was premature, she felt the need to look two, maybe even a dozen steps ahead. If things worked out with Theodore, if everything went perfectly—which she knew wasn't possible—would he even want to get married and have an instant family? She'd met many men over the past year with whom the instant answer was No. And No didn't work for her. She wanted, eventually, to love again. To be loved. To be in a family. She believed in marriage, and she wanted to try it again, but this time with the right man. Could Theodore…?

"Here you go, m'lady," he said as he offered his hand to her. He helped pull her to her feet, her broken foot lifted behind her as if she was a giant flamingo.

She started to hop towards her crutches, but Theodore beat her to them and handed them to her.

"With all of this hopping, I'm going to have really great legs," she said as she got situated with the crutches. "Actually, I'll have one really great leg. It will be all toned. When this is done, it'll be so strong I might actually end up walking in circles."

They made their way to the dining room. It was only a few steps, but Dana still wasn't too sure on her crutches, and her arms were weak with using them.

"Well, you could break your other foot so it will even out," Theodore suggested.

"Not on your life!"

Theodore helped her into her chair, whisking the crutches away so that she could feel somewhat normal. Of course, she had to lift her leg onto the chair next to her to keep the swelling down. She gingerly placed it on the chair.

"Ma! Wait!" Ruby said before running to the living room and grabbing a pillow for the chair. She returned and gently tucked it under Dana's foot.

Dana smiled at her five-year-old's thoughtfulness. "Thanks, Ruby. So. Okay. What's for dinner?"

Theodore turned to the kitchen and said, "Okay, Zach, now!"

Dana watched as Zach very seriously walked into the dining room with a napkin folded over his arm like a French waiter. "Madame, your dinner awakes."

"Awaits," Theodore whispered.

"That's what I said. Your dinner awaits." Then Zach motioned to the kitchen.

"Don't move, Mom! We'll get it for you," said Ruby, then the kids, along with Theodore, scurried into the kitchen and brought out plates and silverware and napkins. Ruby dumped all the silverware in front of Dana, and Zach tossed the napkins onto the table. It seemed their refined manners lasted only so long.

At last, they all sat at the table. Dana nearly started crying all over again. In front of her sat a slice of her spanakopita, the spinach pie. Next to it was a golden chicken breast glistening with a lemon caper sauce. A mixed green salad dotted with balsamic vinegar was served in a side dish, and to top it off, they set a small dish of light creamy chocolate mouse in front of her, drizzled with red raspberry sauce.

"It's a miracle," she said.

"It's dinner," Theodore replied.

"Let's eat it!" Zach cried. He and Ruby climbed up to their seats and immediately everyone started eating.

Chapter 54

"Okay, kiddos," Dana said after they'd had dinner and cleaned up and read stories. "It's time for bed."

Immediately, Ruby threw herself down on the ground and started kicking and screaming.

"Wow," Theodore said.

"It'll pass," Dana said. "Ruby, can you calm down?"

"Noooo! I can't!" she screamed, her little face turning crimson with pure fury.

Over the screaming, she said to Theodore, "This is more of their natural state. You've seen them at their best."

"Is this their worst?" Theodore asked.

Dana didn't need to think about it. "Not even close."

They waited. Ruby screamed. While Ruby screamed and kicked, Zach gathered all of his action figures together into a plastic green container and then took Theodore's hand. Dana watched him do this and felt that familiar lump form in her throat that hinted at oncoming tears. It seemed that as soon as she became a mom she also started crying at every cute thing her kids did, as well as commercials during the holidays. It killed her when a child brought a parent a cup of name-brand coffee.

She cleared her throat to focus herself. She wouldn't cry over a little hand-holding.

"Come on," Zach said to Theodore, loudly enough to be heard over Ruby's screams. "You can put me to bed."

"Uh-uh, big guy," Dana quickly interjected. "*I'll* put you to bed."

"Mom, my bedroom is upstairs. How are you going to get up there?"

"I can do it," Theodore said. "I don't mind."

Dana wasn't sure. For some reason the thought of Theodore putting the kids to bed was a little too much like the things a boyfriend…no…a stepfather would do, and it was too soon for that. She'd spent the last year as a single mom, facing every adversity, doing things that seemed impossible but doing them because she had to.

"Thanks, Theodore, but I really need to do it. You can be my spotter in case anything goes wrong." She looked at Ruby who was still screaming. "You done yet, Ruby?"

Ruby stopped screaming immediately and took a big breath. "I guess so," she said.

"Then let's go." Dana used her crutches to get to the bottom of the stairs. "You might not want to watch this," she said to Theodore. "It's not going to be pretty."

"I'm your spotter, remember?" he said.

Dana nodded. "Okay, kids, who can get up the stairs first?" Those were magic words and the kids took off, practically jumping over one another like tiger cubs to get to the top.

Once there, they looked down at her and Zach said, "Okay, Mom. What are you going to do?"

She took a deep breath, propped the crutches against the wall and then—she crawled.

Chapter 55

Once she got to the top of the stairs, Theodore called up to her, "Are you sure I can't help you?"

"Nope. I got it." She wasn't being purely stubborn. It was important to her to feel like she could still do the things she needed to do for her children. Having Theodore here—or her mom or sister—was nice, but Dana was looking at two months of recovery, and life didn't stop simply because she had a broken foot. It was almost a metaphor in a way. Dana had been through worse, an emotional crippling, and compared to that this physical crippling was just a set back.

She pulled herself to her foot—singular—and hopped to the kids' bedrooms. "Come on guys," she said. "Don't laugh at me. It's what I've got to do."

"I can hop too," Ruby said.

"I can hop more," Zach said.

So the three of them hopped right through their bedtime routine.

Chapter 56

Half an hour later with the kids brushed, pottied, tucked, and sung to, Dana scooted down the stairs on her butt. At the bottom of the stairs, Theodore was waiting, crutches offered to her.

"That was exhausting," she said. "But I think they'll sleep at least until four in the morning."

"Four?" He sounded scared.

"Maybe five. They're early birds." She took the crutches from him. "I'm really hurting," she said. "I needed to do that, but man, it's exhausting, I'm just so tired I could…"

She didn't finish her sentence because Theodore had leaned in, pulled her gently to him, and kissed her. She didn't even need the crutches for balance. After a moment of which she was certain he had stolen her breath from her, he gently set the crutches against the wall and then scooped her up into her arms, broken foot extended.

"What are you doing?" she gasped.

"I'm carrying you to the couch. Just think of it as an extension of our wedding night in Vegas, only this line here, the line separating the breezeway from the living room, this is the threshold."

She snuggled against him. She had to admit that A) it felt nice to be held, and B) she was delighted that she was either skinny enough or he was strong enough to actually be able to lift her. "You're carrying me over the threshold?" she asked.

"Damn straight." And with only a hint of a stumble, he carried her straight into the living room and placed her gently on the couch. "What do you need? Frozen peas? Pillows? Vicodin?"

Dana shook her head. Her bad foot was on the inside of the couch, resting on the pillows, and though it hurt more than she cared to think about, her mind wanted to think of other things instead. She didn't want to think forty steps ahead or analyze Theodore's intentions or whether she could trust him. She just wanted to stop thinking about her foot, and more than that, she wanted him. Even if only for a little bit. She tugged on his hand.

"Come here," she said.

"Are you sure?"

She nodded. Currently, she had two different kinds of throbs going on. One was her foot, but the other…oh, the other… "Would you mind just getting on top of me and kissing me for a while? You know, pretend that you're a teenager again?" She tried not to think about "dry humping", but she was fully prepared to do that if he was.

"Not a problem," he said with a smile, and then crawled gently on top of her. They both started laughing. It felt ridiculous, yet somehow really nice to feel the weight of him against her. They adjusted their bodies, and he seemed to be very careful of not jarring her foot, which was still perched in the air on a tower of pillows. "I'm glad you're flexible," he said and kissed her throat.

"Oh, I'm very flexible," she said. "And if this actually were the evening of our Las Vegas adventure, and you had really just carried me over the threshold, and I didn't have this broken foot, I would show you just how flexible I am."

He kissed her throat again. Then he moved infinitesimally upward and began a series of kisses that started out soft and sweet and then deepened and lengthened. Dana opened herself up to his kisses. It really was a sort of opening up, or letting down of barriers. There was the story of Sleeping Beauty and how she was surrounded by a forest of thorns. Dana had surrounded her heart with thorns, but this Theodore, this quirky man who loved food and Elvis had, almost from the start, been able to bring down her barriers effortlessly.

His lips reached hers. There was a slight pause with his lips poised over hers. She nodded. He kissed her. Softly and then with more urgency. Their kisses deepened. She ran her hands down his back, to his belt, felt the weight of him against her, and that familiar—but almost forgotten—hardness between them.

"I know this is cheesy, but I want you so much," he said.

She couldn't say anything. She just nodded.

His hands moved under her shirt, over the lace of her bra. She yearned for him to slip his hands under the bra, or behind her back and free her from that barrier that separated them too.

"Will the kids wake up?" he asked quietly.

She shook her head and arched her back to allow him access to her bra strap. It took several tries and she giggled, much like the teenager he made her feel like, until the bra snapped open, and she was free beneath his hands.

"Unbutton," she said.

His fingers quickly moved over the buttons of her shirt, the loose bra still covering her breasts. Quicker than she thought possible, her shirt was off and the bra tossed aside, and finally, finally his mouth was all over her. On her lips, her neck and then to her great relief, on her nipples. He kissed her lovingly, gently at first and she moaned lightly. While he kissed one breast, he massaged the other with his hand, cupping her, holding her. She felt awash in heat, and a hunger she didn't know she had unfurled within her. She wanted all of him. She wanted their bodies naked and pressed together. She wanted to experiment with positions she didn't even know were physically possible. She wanted to kiss him and taste him and take him inside her.

"I wish I could make love to you," he said.

"I know," she said, breathless. "But we can't." It took everything within her to admit that to him.

"The kids?" he asked.

She stopped kissing him for a moment. "No! My foot! I should probably have a cast on first. I don't want to bump my foot." Then an image appeared in her mind, and she started laughing.

"What is it?" he asked, smiling.

"I just had an image of me trying to be all sexy with a gigantic cast on. I mean, how could we even…how would you…?"

"We would manage," he said firmly. "Trust me. We *will* manage." He kissed her softly again. "I'll get off you. I must be killing you."

"You're killing me all right, but it's not the weight of you."

He carefully crawled off her, adjusted her foot on the pillows, and then handed Dana her bra and shirt. "Put these on. I'll be back in a second."

She decided to skip the bra entirely and just put on her shirt. There was something sensual about going braless and feeling her skin rub against the fabric. God, she really was horny, she laughed to herself.

After a moment, he came back with a bag of peas, a glass of water and her pain pills. "You've got to take these," he said.

Dana glanced at him. He was holding her prescription bottle in one hand with the glass of water and the peas in the other. "I assume you mean the pills. I'm not a huge fan of frozen peas. Cooked…maybe."

"Yes. I mean the pills." He handed them to her and she took them.

"Okay," she said. "Phew. That was fun. Now what?" She wasn't talking about the medication.

Theodore seemed to consider that. "Are you sure your kids won't wake up?"

"Yes…"

He smiled and ran to the light switch and turned it off. For a moment, Dana was blinded by the sudden darkness. "What are you doing?" she asked.

"Shhh…" he said. She felt his hands on her waist and then he unbuttoned and unzipped her jeans.

"No!" she cried.

"You don't want me to?" He kissed the softness of her belly, drew his tongue across her panty line. "I'll stop. I don't want to pressure you." He kissed just under the line of her lace. "But if you want me to, I will."

"I do want you to. I just don't want my pants to get stuck on my foot." She tried to say it without laughing, but it was hard. She loved the feel of him near her, kissing her, and she suddenly wanted all that she could get from him…even though she felt slightly ridiculous.

"Your pants won't get stuck. They won't need to," Theodore said. He pulled her pants down to her knees, and then, kneeling on the floor by the couch, he began to kiss her, softly, his mouth warm and wet, down the inside of her leg, over the fabric of her panties.

"Oh, God," she said, and then surprised herself by whispering, "Please."

With that, he pulled her panties down to her knees too, and then kissed her all over again, until Dana couldn't breathe or think or do anything but feel swept away by pleasure and, yes, maybe even love.

Chapter 57

Dana spoke before she really thought about it. "I think maybe I've fallen in love with him," she said to Valerie.

They were on their way home from the foot specialist, and Dana was sporting a very new and very green cast, and the prescription that she'd be in the cast for four weeks, and then an air cast for another six weeks and then maybe, *maybe* she'd be able to go without one.

All morning she'd been unable to focus on anything besides the memory of Theodore's kisses, but there was something else worrying her too. Something that was far more distressing—the idea that she had never felt as relaxed and comfortable and vibrantly alive than when Theo was within three feet of her. Or kissing her wherever he could.

She had a quick flashback to her jeans twisted around her legs and the man right between her…well. She shook her head. "I really think this is love," she continued. "I've never felt like this before. It's worse than being a teenager."

"Surely you don't mean you've fallen in love with the doctor. After the pain he put you through?" Valerie said.

Dana was glad the kids were in school and daycare so that they didn't have to see her go through that. The doctor, though very nice, had to reset her foot. It meant bending it painfully while wrapping her foot in the casting material.

"If we don't get it in the right position, it won't heal correctly," he'd said, followed by, "I hate to tell you this, but this is going to hurt." And it had. Dana had bit her lip and tried to breathe through the pain, but she'd cried anyway.

"No, I am not in love with the doctor. I mean Theodore."

Valerie laughed. "And you're sure it's love and not just being really grateful for having a non-self-delivered orgasm for the first time in over a year?" Dana had told Valerie all of the details of last night.

"It's the first one in *many* years," Dana corrected. She checked behind her and saw that the twins were, indeed, still deep asleep. "My sex life with Paul was just one of our many problems."

Valerie nodded. "So…what's different? How do you know?"

"Is that really your reaction? Aren't you going to say, 'Dana, knock it off. It's too early. You barely know the guy'?"

"Do you want me to say that?"

"I don't know," Dana said. She tried to lift her foot, surprised by the weight of it. "This cast is going to be a pain."

"Everything's a pain," Valerie said. She sounded grumpy. "I will say those things if you want me to, sis, but the truth is, I don't know if I believe them. I mean, shoot, you're thirty-seven, I'm thirty-five. We both have two kids. We've both been married. College is a lifetime ago. I think if you were saying this and you were twenty-five, I'd tell you to slow down, but now? If I were ever out in the dating world again, I think I'd know within five minutes of meeting a guy if he was worth my time. No. Two. I'd know in two. So if you think you love this guy, then I say go for it. But just, you know, let's do a police check on him first. Scratch that. I'm sure Dad has already called in some of his old Guard buddies. Theodore's got to be clean."

Dana noticed that as Valerie drove the speed was increasing.

"Are you mad about something? Your voice is getting that edgy thing again. I'm sorry I asked you to drive me. I know I've been asking a lot of you lately. And…don't be pissed. I'm not criticizing you…but you're going almost eighty."

Valerie checked the speedometer. "Shit," she whispered and then decelerated. "I am angry, but not at you." She was quiet for a time.

"You aren't thinking of getting back in the dating game are you?" Dana asked gently. She'd noticed the strain that seemed to be growing between her and Vick.

They'd always been such a compatible and fun loving couple. Then when Valerie was pregnant, things started to change. She had a tough pregnancy and was sick all the time and then they'd found out they were having twins. Since the twins were born, she was constantly sleep-deprived and often said that she felt like she didn't even get to have her own body any more. It belonged to her ever-nursing boys and to a husband who wanted to be intimate with her. What *she* wanted was to sleep and not be poked, suckled, and prodded for, as she said, about ten years.

"I'm sorry I'm all bitchy. I'm actually jealous of you," Valerie admitted.

Dana was shocked. Her happily married, beautiful, smart, younger sister was jealous of *her*? "Why? What do I have that you don't? Do you have any idea how hard and lonely and horrible this year has been?"

"I know. I know. It's crazy, right? But you always seem to have the more interesting life. I mean, you had your time with Paul and then that drama, and then working, and a business, and your kids are older, and now you've met this great guy who is perfect for you and if you love him I say go for it…and geez…what's next for you? The pot of gold at the end of the rainbow?"

Valerie turned the car to take their exit to Coopersville. They slowed and turned onto the small road that led to the downtown and passed rolling farmland and then modest houses.

"I know I sound crazy," Valerie continued. "Especially since you've now got a broken foot and how on earth could I be jealous of that? I just want…ugh. I just want someone to take care of me for a while. I just want something of my own besides just being a mom and a wife. I feel like I'm disappearing."

Dana was quiet for a bit. Valerie passed a series of churches, and then the Main Street of Coopersville. She didn't want to say the wrong thing. And she wanted, deeply, to help her sister.

When they finally drove up to Dana's house and Valerie put the car in park, Dana said, "I know what you mean, Val. Completely. If I could take care of you right now, I would. After my foot heals…let's go to a spa or something. But maybe there's something we can do. Maybe we could figure out something you could do that's just for you. Just you. Not Vick or the kids or even me. You need it. Come inside, bring the boys, and we'll have coffee, which I will make for you. I feel a little more confident with this indestructible cast. And we'll brainstorm. And I promise not to talk about all my own stuff for a change. We can just talk about you."

Dana wasn't sure if it was the right thing to say or not, but Valerie turned to her and smiled. "I've already started a list of things I want to do," she said happily. "And some of them actually do involve you, just in a different way. You agree to what I'm asking and we can go back to talking about you and Theodore and planning your wedding."

Valerie shut off the ignition. "Oh. Wait. I forgot. You already had a wedding with the guy. Guess this one will be just for show."

The idea seemed to lift Valerie's spirits. Dana didn't know what to think, except that the idea of standing at an altar with Theodore for a second time was actually starting to really appeal to her. Of course it was completely crazy. They were just…what…dating? Yeah. Dating. It wasn't as if they were really even talking about getting married. But the idea of an event to plan seemed to suddenly give Valerie some sort of electric shock therapy or something.

Dana shrugged her shoulders and helped Valerie inside. She still had about thirty seconds to think through things before her sister took over entirely. Still, she thought it might be just the thing her sister needed.

Who was she kidding? It might be just the thing Dana needed, to have a man in her life that she was deeply attracted to and connected to in a way that was both mysterious and strangely fun. And it might be a good thing for the kids and Theo too. She had almost convinced herself by the time she and her sister walked into the kitchen.

The hard part, she thought, would be convincing Theodore that sooner was better than later.

Chapter 58

The success of the opening day of Foodies was not a fluke, Theodore was certain of it. Foodies was going to be a hit. Sure, there was the favorable review in the paper and the local news channel, but there was something even stronger. By day three, they already had regulars coming in, and Angelique knew their names by heart. She'd told Theodore and Mike that since Mike would be heading back to Detroit soon—wouldn't he?—they needed to hire some support staff, so they'd taken in two students from the local art college. One looked like a blonde Betty Page and the other looked like Frankenstein's offspring. Both of them fit in nicely with the ever-changing clientele they were attracting.

Now, at the end of another long and successful day, they were counting down the till, restocking, and Angelique was asking questions.

"Which one of you is getting married first?" she asked. "Cause I need to put it in my calendar. I am an awfully busy woman, as is my wife, and if you want me to attend not one, but two weddings, then you need to give me some warning. None of this flying off to Las Vegas rigmarole. I am a woman who likes to plan."

Theodore wasn't sure if he or Mike were choking. One of them was making loud coughing noises. Ah. It turned out to be Mike.

"Woman," he finally managed. "Woman" was his new term of endearment for Angelique. She allowed it. "You must be crazy. I am not getting married again. Not ever. No way. No how. Why, I am just getting back into the swing of things and you are absolutely crazy if…"

Angelique just stared at him.

"We're planning on a summer wedding," he said shyly. "Mavis wants it when her garden is in bloom."

Now Theodore was the one choking. "Are you serious, Mike? Seriously? You asked Mavis to marry you? You just got divorced…for the third time! What happened?"

Angelique answered before Mike could say a word. "It's as plain as an unpowdered donut what has happened. It's called Love, Theodore. And you know a little bit about that. It's what you're feeling for your woman friend, you know, that broken one. The one with the clipped wing."

"Foot."

"*Wing.* I was speaking in metaphors."

"Never use a metaphor on a man," Theodore said. "We don't speak that language."

"Why do you think I'm a lesbian?"

Theodore shook his head. Some things he just didn't need to comment on.

Angelique continued, "Anyway, I'm outta here. You fellas can lock up, yes? I'll plan on a long day tomorrow since it's the day before

Thanksgiving. Do you plan on selling special side dishes and dips from the deli?"

Mike didn't answer. He seemed to be in some sort of waking coma where he couldn't speak, probably due to admitting he had plans to marry his nearly sixty-years-old girlfriend.

Theodore considered. "I actually hadn't thought about it."

"See? Love."

"It's not love!" he said and then immediately thought… well…. maybe it was. Something was going on. Something different than anything he'd experienced before.

Before, with Sarah and even with other girlfriends, when he envisioned his life, he had to force them into it. Mostly, he just imagined his own life in a slightly different space, still on his own, still working. But now, now something had shifted and when he tried to imagine where he would be in two years, in five, in ten, somehow, he saw himself in a small house in Coopersville with his family, and that family started with Dana and her two kids.

"I'll make some dips tonight," he said, finally.

Angelique nodded and headed for the door. "Make sure you don't do anything stupid," she said and was gone before Theodore could ask her what on earth she was talking about.

Sometimes it was better to not know.

Chapter 59

How was it that one day you had a quiet life and you were content, and the next that very same life seemed painfully empty and quiet?

Theodore stood in his apartment looking around. He didn't have any pets because Sarah had been allergic. His home was just the way he'd left it in the morning. Why wouldn't it be? There was no one else there to change anything. There was his coffee maker still half-filled from the morning. There were the socks he had taken off last night under the coffee table when he'd tried to read a few minutes before falling asleep. The lights came on and off with timers. Theodore himself might have been run on timers. His kitchen was clean, the bathroom had the razor by the sink the way he'd left it; his bed was made and unslept in. His home was an empty shell. Now, even his walls were nearly bare after removing the pictures of him and Sarah. He actually didn't mind that as those pictures were of a reality that almost was and one he didn't want.

He missed…how funny to think it…he missed the chaos that was Dana's world. Her home was warm and vibrant and alive. His home was cold and sterile and desperately needed some love.

Theodore, for that matter, needed some love too. He knew just where to find it, and it was only a half hour away. Still, he had dips and side dishes to make and after he relaxed and ate, he'd have to go back into downtown Grand Rapids and use the professional kitchen that was located in the back of their store. He probably should've just stayed there and done it, but for some reason, he'd needed to come home. Maybe to discover that there was nothing waiting for him here.

He opened the refrigerator and stared at the nearly empty contents. Dana's fridge was stuffed and ready to feed a family. His fridge could barely offer him more than a turkey sandwich and some forlorn olives. He reached for the sandwich makings when he heard a familiar tap, tap, tap on his door.

Immediately, his stomach sank. Only one person tap, tap, tapped like that, and he thought he'd never see her again.

He opened the door and there she stood—Sarah, his ex-fiancée, wearing a matching pink skirt with a jacket and pink heels and, for some reason, stockings that had seams on the back. Something wasn't quite right here.

"Hello, Theo-adore," she said in a sing-songy voice. She pushed him aside from the door, effectively forcing herself in. "My, what you have done with the place? It looks absolutely…the same!" She laughed and Theodore felt his skin prickle.

"What are you doing here, Sarah?" he said, not bothering to keep the edge out of his voice.

"Well, why shouldn't I be here, silly? I've come to help you prepare for, you know, our Thanksgiving. My whole family is coming and they are expecting the feast that you promised." Her voice was odd, strangely upbeat, but somehow laced with a threat of some sort.

"Sarah, I'm not..." Theodore didn't know what to say. "I'm not cooking for your family for this Thanksgiving, or any future Thanksgiving. Now, your family is nice and all but you and I...we're not..."

"Oh, you're so ridiculously stubborn," she said, cutting him off. "Fine. I'm sorry I was a little pushy. And now you can be sorry for being an idiot. The wedding is back on. I haven't told any of my family because I knew you'd come to your senses eventually."

Theodore didn't respond, so Sarah apparently took this as some sort of agreement. "And now we can have make-up sex and forget this ever happened, okay? That's what you men hold out for, isn't it? Make up sex. So, fine. Whatever. Here."

With that she unzipped her outfit and before Theodore could stop her, she stood before him in a black lacy negligee that pushed her breasts up fiercely. Now the stocking made sense. He noticed how flat her stomach was, the curve of her breasts, the shape of her legs and then remembered Angelique's warning to not do something stupid. It wasn't hard. Literally. It. Wasn't. Hard. Mostly, he just wanted her gone.

He didn't want the sharp lines of her body or to have sex be used as some kind of weapon. He wanted...Dana. And the softness of her stomach and the curve of her inner thigh, and mostly he wanted Dana looking at him when he leaned in to kiss her.

"Sarah..." he began.

"What? What the fuck, Theodore? You're not possibly telling me 'no' are you?"

"No," he said softly. And then a little louder, "No, Sarah. I don't want to have make-up sex with you. I don't want to have sex with you at all."

Sarah reached for her dress and tugged it back on angrily. "So that guy you met in Vegas…?"

"I didn't meet a guy."

"Whatever. That chick, whoever. What is she a showgirl or something? Does she have bigger boobs than I do? Because I can guarantee you, hers aren't real. And mine are. And this," she grabbed one of her breasts and shook it at him.

He was a little stunned that a woman could actually shake a breast, but she apparently could.

"This, baby, is real." She tucked her boobs into her top and zipped it up.

Theodore lowered his eyes.

And then he heard a peculiar thing. He heard Sarah sit down and then what sounded like sobbing. He looked up at her. Sure enough, she was crying. Great big man-tears were coursing down her cheeks, and she was sobbing these huge sobs that made her sound like a mule. In heat.

Theodore didn't know what to do so he went over to her and patted her shoulder.

"I don't want to have sex with you either, Theodore," she said. "And I'm sorry I came over her. It's so pathetic. I just couldn't bear to tell my family that we aren't getting married. They're convinced I'm a lesbian and that my womb is a dustbin. They don't think any man will ever want to marry me and when you asked…"

"Actually, you asked me," Theodore gently corrected. "Rather, you kind of told me."

"Whatever. I just don't want to be alone and, you know, dusty."

Theodore grabbed a tissue for her and dabbed at her cheeks. "You won't be alone, Sarah. You won't. Just give it a little time. Tell your family whatever you need to," he paused as he thought about that, "except that I'm gay. I'm not gay. Or, that's fine. Tell them that. But I'm not involved with a man…just so you know. And she's not a showgirl. She makes jam, and she's a single mom."

"You've left me for Betty Crocker?" she said, the sobs quieting now to a whimper.

"Sort of," he said. "I can't explain it, Sarah, but I fit with her. It's easy. Effortless. I don't know if it's fate or kismet or what, but she feels like home to me."

Sarah nodded as if she understood. "They always say that in romantic movies and then right after that one of the characters gets cancer and dies. Not that I'm wishing that on you. You really are a pretty decent guy. And we did have some fun times together, didn't we?"

Theodore tried to remember some fun times, but couldn't exactly pinpoint one. Still, though, there were times when one shouldn't be honest. "We did."

She nodded, wiped the makeup from her face with the back of her hands, and blew her nose loudly into the tissue. "I'll tell them you left me for another woman. I'll tell them you cheated. I'll tell them you broke my heart. That should get me at least through Christmas." She stood and grabbed her bag.

"Is any of that true?" he asked her. "Did I break your heart? Do you think I cheated on you?" He didn't know quite why, but he felt it was important that he know.

"No, Theodore, you didn't. I don't think I ever gave you my heart to break in the first place. I'm not saying that to be mean…I just…"

"I know," he agreed. "Take care, Sarah. And I'm sorry."

She nodded. "Okay then. I'm off. We'll probably never see each other again." She paused as if to consider that. "It's funny isn't it? How one minute you're with someone and the next your life goes on without them in it." She kissed his cheek and then left.

After a moment, it seemed that even her perfume had left along with her. How quickly someone could move out of your life.

Theodore agreed that it was strange. It was also strange that one moment, someone was a stranger to you and the next you knew that you couldn't live without them. Thanksgiving, he thought, couldn't come quickly enough.

Chapter 60

Dana and Valerie talked all afternoon, coming up with a plan of attack for Val. Well, not a plan of *attack*, exactly. Mostly it seemed that Dana's sister was just looking for something to get her mind off her nipples.

Dana was afraid at first that Valerie really was going to plan an ambush wedding for her and Theodore; her idea, in comparison, was actually quite harmless. It seemed that Valerie wanted to get involved and help Dana run her business. At first, Dana had felt possessive of it, but then, listening to Valerie's suggestions, she realized that her sister might just have a very keen business sense. And Val would have time when Dana didn't. She'd cancelled this week of classes because of her broken foot, but next week, she'd be prepping students for their final essays, and she'd be buried under paperwork. She'd also have to take extra time getting to and from classes in the ice and snow on crutches. So, Val's meltdown seemed to come just at the right time.

She'd left Dana's house a woman transformed. Dana understood. It was important as a woman to have something of your own, something beyond being a wife and a mom, though both of those things were great. She'd learned the hard way that when you gave up too much of yourself, you eventually disappeared, and she didn't want that to happen to her sister.

Now, Dana sat in her living room. She'd managed to get the kids tucked into bed. They'd developed a system. Zach would help drag Dana's crutches up the stairs and Ruby would follow them from behind, making sure Dana didn't roll down the stairs—although, Dana knew, if she actually did roll down the stairs, she'd roll right over Ruby. Once at the top of the stairs, she could lean against the wall and hop to her foot. Then she could use the crutches.

The hardest part was when Ruby had cried, "But I want you to pick me up!" And Dana had had to explain to her that she couldn't physically pick her up for some time. The disappointment on Ruby's face had cut straight into her heart. But they'd got through it. And if they could get through this, they could get through much more.

She put her feet on the coffee table and propped the foot in the cast up on a stack of couch cushions. She sipped her wine. Her mind drifted to Theodore. He was coming to Thanksgiving the day after tomorrow, and she was more excited than she thought she had a right to be. It seemed that after a year of waiting, after more of feeling lost and like she was drifting, she finally felt anchored to life. She felt like she belonged. She was scared. Timid. Unsure. But she wanted these feelings to go on. And she wanted Theodore beside her.

What she was feeling *was* love. Real love. A quiet kind of love, one in which it felt like recognizing and old friend with an "Oh, there you are" type feeling.

She set her wine down on the coffee table, closed her eyes and slept. She did not dream. She didn't need to.

Chapter 61

Wednesday passed in a blur. The kids destroyed every clean room in the house. They covered it with toys and crayons and practiced letters.

"That's not a Q," Zach said. "That's an R." He was trying to teach Ruby how to write letters. Ruby actually knew more letters than Zach did, and this caused a few fights that Dana had had to intervene on.

She tried to cook. She was going to make pie crusts and applesauce. Prep dinner rolls and side dishes, but by four o'clock, she hadn't done a single thing, and her foot was throbbing. She could call her sister for help, but her sister was a terrible cook. She might be able to take the business to the next level, but she wouldn't be allowed to touch the food. And Dana also didn't want to call her parents. They'd wanted to take everyone to the Grand Buffet. Dana had insisted she'd work out a plan. She'd call in a caterer, she'd told them, when secretly she was just planning on cooking everything herself.

When her family and Theodore saw the fantastic feast she'd managed to prepare while on crutches, they'd have stood and applauded.

"You're #1!" her mom cheered in her mind.

"You should've been in the Guard!" her dad cried, both arms in the air, cheering. It was a little ridiculous the things she had her parents say in her mind.

Now, Dana realized that with bedtime a few hours away and the idea of driving to the grocery store nearly unthinkable, there was only one thing she could do. Funny that she hadn't thought of it earlier. She called Theo.

"Thank you for calling Foodies. This is Angelique. And how may I help you today?"

Dana smiled. She almost felt like this woman actually could help her. "Angelique, this is Dana Kupiac calling for…"

"Are you the Dana Kupiac of Dana's Delights?"

Dana was about to answer, but didn't have much of a chance.

Angelique continued, "When I heard that name, I must say I thought that you sold intimates. You know, lacy underthings and crotchless panties and all that jazz. I was very happy to find out that you actually sold homemade butterscotch sauce and jams. You don't sell crotchless panties, do you?"

"Uh…"

"No worries. I'll find some online. You're calling for Theodore, aren't you? You having trouble getting ready for tomorrow? I'll send Theodore over to your house with what's left of the stuff here. He cooked all night last night. Seems he couldn't get his mind off some woman."

Dana felt her throat constrict, until Angelique burst out into laughter. "No worries. That woman he's thinking about is you. Do me a favor," Angelique's voice lowered to a hush, "say yes." And then she screamed,

"Theodore! Your woman needs your help! Grab some of that smoked salmon and those crackers!"

Dana heard the phone clunk down and then footsteps. There was a door chime ringing and then she thought she heard a train whistle of all things and then just before she was going to hang up the phone, she heard Theo's voice say her name.

"Yes," she said immediately.

Theodore cleared his throat. "Hey, you."

"Hey," she said. Then felt foolish for immediately saying "yes" to him, almost as if that woman had put a spell on her or something. "Who was that?" she asked. She had to know.

"She's just our store manager. And an absolute genius. And she tells fortunes. Be careful. Did she tell you anything interesting?"

Dana hesitated. "Yes," she said again. "She told me to say yes." There was an awkward pause between them, which after a moment Theodore broke.

"Uh…did you need some help? Are you calling to cancel tomorrow? Is everything okay? Are you hurt?"

His flurry of questions confused her…and somehow she still felt propelled to say yes, even though that was really only the answer to half of the questions. "I don't know if it's as serious as needing help but, yes, okay. I could use some help. Or some company. Which is ridiculous because I know you're coming over tomorrow, and you guys must be absolutely swamped and…"

"No, we're not!" Dana heard Angelique's voice bellow from somewhere in the store.

"I'm on my way," Theodore said. "Hey. Don't let this freak you out, but I've missed you."

Dana smiled. "Yes," she said.

Chapter 62

It took twenty-seven minutes to get from downtown Grand Rapids to Dana's house in Coopersville if one hit most of the green lights and obeyed the speed limits. Tonight, it took Theodore nineteen minutes. It wasn't smart, he knew, but Dana needed help and he could help her. It made him feel manly. Sure, the help he could offer came in the form of cheesecake and assorted appetizers, but still, she needed help, she called, and he was ready.

He pulled into her driveway and ran up the walkway. Before he even got to the door, it swung open, and there stood Dana, on crutches, green cast shining, if a cast could shine in the dark.

"Hi," he said and stood just outside the door. A brisk wind blew through the trees, rustling the last of the leaves that still clung to the treetops. He gently took a step forward, leaned in and kissed her. "You're shivering," he said.

"It's not the cold that's making me shiver," she said. "Come in, Theo. Please." She turned on her crutches and let him inside. "I'm getting pretty good on these things. By Christmas time I should be able to ice skate with them."

"Please don't," he said. "You don't want to break your legs as well as your foot." He paused and listened. "Are the kids asleep?"

"Yep. Honestly, I now feel entirely foolish for calling you. I'm just having a freak out because tomorrow is Thanksgiving, and my family is coming over, and I told them that it wouldn't be a big deal and that I was going to order in a lot of the food. And they're planning on helping in the morning anyway. It isn't like I have to do everything alone. I mean, I can, you know. I can do everything alone. I don't need anyone. I'm perfectly capable of taking care of myself and the kids and cooking a turkey dinner even on crutches. I could do it in a wheelchair if I had to because if I've learned anything this year it's that when you're a mom, you do anything you have to. You don't have a choice. You just do it. I pay the mortgage. I work. I make sure the kids have clothes and toys and love. Lots of love. And I work on having a good relationship with their dad even though I'm furious at him for moving to Ohio and starting over and not having time for the kids anymore."

As she talked, Theodore gently took her crutches from her and leaned them against the wall, holding her hand so she wouldn't lose balance. Then he looped his arms around her waist.

She paused for a second as if registering the closeness of their bodies and then continued. "And I wasn't even ready to date. Okay. Maybe I was ready. But I don't need to. You know? You understand what I'm saying. I don't need you. I don't."

"Okay," Theodore said. "Is it okay if I actually do need you?"

She smiled at him. "Yes! Thank God!"

And then Theodore couldn't stop himself anymore. They could talk about everything later. They could figure out their lives and details and emotions later. There would be details, like how to tell the kids, and how to combine their houses, but Theodore was certain they could work them out.

So he did the most natural thing in the world. He just held onto her and kissed her. He wanted to do so much more. He wanted to wake up with her in the morning and snuggle in with her at night. He wanted to make love to her. He wanted all of her. He wanted to cook with her and for her.

Until then, he could only kiss her, but for now it was enough.

Chapter 63

Dana checked her face in the mirror. Her lips were plumped from kissing. She looked like Steven Tyler only, hopefully, a little more attractive and a lot more feminine. Every day she was feeling more and more like a teenager. It wasn't a bad thing.

She'd so wanted to make love to Theodore, to share with him that level of intimacy and not just because she'd gone over a year without sex. Longer, since she and Paul had stopped having sex months before he left her. So, she wanted to sleep with Theodore, but at the same time she was terrified of losing this…newness. She'd been married and knew that with time, passion cooled, could even become arctic and she just didn't know if she could do that again. Where was the guarantee? How did she know that what happened between her and Paul wouldn't happen between her and Theodore? It was terrifying!

Still, she tried not to think about it. She enjoyed his kisses. The way he held her, balanced her so she didn't fall. She liked that he ran his hands through her hair and then down her back.

He kissed her neck and her eyelids and, of course, her lips, giving them a little bite.

"We can't," she said at last. "I mean, we could, but I just want…I want our first time together to be totally relaxed and I don't want to worry that the kids will walk in." She looked at him, trying to read his expression. "I'm afraid that if we decide to have a relationship, that's what it's going to be like, you know. I've got kids. We won't have hours to spend in bed with each other, not unless they're with their grandparents or their dad. And I don't know if I can have you sleep over. And I don't…"

"Dana, it's okay," he said quietly and pulled her in for a hug. "You're a package deal. You have kids. I know that. And I actually think seeing you with them makes me love you all the more."

He loved her. He said he *loved* her. It seemed there was a reason for the cliché. The cliché happened; she felt her heart *skip*. She was almost afraid to ask. "Did you mean to just say that? What you said?"

He pulled away and looked at her and smiled. "I didn't consciously plan to say that out loud, no. But I do mean it. It's crazy, I know. Please don't think I'm a stalker or anything. I know it's really fast. And I know I'm just out of a relationship, but that relationship was wrong and you're…well…you're *right*."

"It is fast," she agreed.

"But it's also effortless."

"And it feels right."

"I don't know…" he said, still holding her. "I think we might've been onto something in Las Vegas. Maybe some part of us knew that the whole 'let's pretend to get married' thing wasn't just an act. Maybe…maybe it was practice."

After that, Dana couldn't speak. She was too busy making out like a sixteen-year-old, except she was thirty-seven, divorced, and standing on one foot. It didn't matter. She felt young and light as a wish.

Chapter 64

Theodore slept on the couch and was awakened in a peculiar way. There was a lightsaber aimed right at his heart, held by a very intense six-year-old boy. "You will not win against the Resistance. We will not let you!"

"Uh…" Theodore rubbed his eyes.

Zach put the lightsaber down and smiled at him. "Hi, Theo. Guess what? Mom's stuck in the turkey!"

Theodore wasn't sure which was weirder…being threatened that he wouldn't survive the Resistance, or the image of Dana stuck inside a turkey. "That sounds serious," he said, figuring that was a safe answer. "Where is she?"

"Over there," Zach said and reached for his hand. He led Theo into the kitchen where, indeed, Dana seemed to either be having intimate relations with the turkey, or she was trying to help it deliver a baby.

"It's. Frozen. And I can't…" She struggled to twist something. She had her leg bent on a chair for leverage, and the crutches were at her side. "Can't…get the bag…out." She gave another tug and there was a slight pop and then the bag of turkey innards flew across the kitchen and landed against the wall.

Ruby screamed.

Zach turned on his lightsaber and leapt at the frozen giblets. "I'll kill it, Mom!" He whacked it before they could stop him.

Theodore started laughing.

"Oh, my God. I'm so sorry," Dana said.

"It's not a problem," Theodore said, walking over to the partially frozen bag and scooping it up into the trash. "I'll clean this up, and you work on the turkey."

"Mom, was that the turkey's baby?" Ruby asked.

"No, Ruby. The turkey did not have a baby."

"So, we're not going to eat a baby for Thanksgiving?"

"No, sweetie. We're not. We're eating plain old turkey," Dana responded.

Theodore wondered if he was actually going to eat the turkey now. His stomach was turning a little.

"There's spray disinfectant under the sink," Dana said to him.

Theodore nodded, grabbed a handful of paper towels and began to clean.

"Are you staying for Thanksgiving?" Zach asked Theodore.

"I am, yes. Is that okay with you?"

Zach considered it. "Only if you do a battle with me."

"Zach, don't make conditions with someone. That's not nice," Dana said.

"What? Mom, it's not an addition. I'm just saying that he can stay if he plays with me. *You're* making him cook."

"I will battle with you," Theodore said. "In between battling with the turkey."

"Oh," Dana said. "This battle is done." She held the turkey up and looked at it. "Turkey, I hate to tell you this, but carnivores won."

Ruby said, "Yay! Carnivores won! Carnivores won!"

Theodore smiled to himself. Usually, he woke up to coffee and NPR. He had to say that this way was a lot more entertaining.

Chapter 65

After Dana had scrubbed her hands and arms as if she was a surgeon preparing for surgery, she made a fresh pot of coffee. She hadn't told Theodore the time yet and wondered if he had any idea that it was 5:30 in the morning. Her kiddos were early birds.

She hopped over to the cupboard and grabbed the grounds then hopped back to the sink. She'd found that the crutches were too cumbersome in the kitchen. Hopping probably wasn't the safest thing in the world, but it sure was the quickest. She filled the pot with water and loaded in the coffee grounds.

Theodore was in the front room playing a lightsaber battle with Zach and taking breaks every now and then from Ruby's tea party. Dana liked the sound of their laughter and the occasional sound effects both Zach and Theodore provided for the lightsabers.

Paul had been much more reserved with the children. He was a good father, strong and protective, but he was guarded in so many ways. And she felt such sorrow when she thought about his choice. He'd called her yesterday to say that his wife was on bed rest, and they wouldn't be coming to Michigan for Thanksgiving, after all, so he couldn't see the kids. What made Dana even sadder was that the kids had stopped asking when they were going to see their dad. So to hear them laughing and playing, well, Dana felt her heart growing just a little bit.

She replayed their conversation from last night. What was it he had said? That maybe their performance in Las Vegas at the wedding chapel hadn't been just for fun…maybe it had been practice? Practice for what?

Who was she kidding? She knew the answer to that question. Practice for the real thing. The connection she felt for him was just that—the real thing. She could argue with herself that it was too soon, that they were strangers, but she just didn't have the energy. She loved him. It was crazy and maybe foolish, but that was the reality.

She pressed "go" on the coffee maker, and even the percolating coffee seemed happy.

Chapter 66

The morning passed by in a blur of cooking preparation. "Tell me what you want from me and I'll do it," Theodore said. "I'm actually a pretty good cook."

"I'm not surprised," Dana said. "Thanks for coming over yesterday…and being willing to help with today. I don't know what I was thinking. There's no way I could've prepared this on my own. I can't even lift the turkey."

"You did lift it. Into the sink. But it might be hard to hop around with it."

Dana smiled. "Seriously. Thank you."

"And thank you for inviting me. I would be in my apartment, heating up a frozen dinner and doing inventory if you hadn't called. So really, *you* rescued *me*." He paused and rubbed his hands together. "Okay then. Turkey is in. What do we do next? Are we going traditional Midwestern, where I cook a mean broccoli and cheese casserole, or do we go gourmet where I make stuffed mushrooms with pine nuts. I've brought enough groceries for practically anything we can think of."

Dana considered it. "Is there any way we could do both? Like a marriage of class and something to honor our Midwestern roots? I mean, it is Thanksgiving and shouldn't we at least have one dish that comes out of a can?"

"My broccoli cheese casserole is made with Velveeta. Does that count?"

"Score!" Dana laughed. She pointed to the knives and told Theodore he could get chopping. She set the kids up with a movie and then she and Theodore worked in a companionable silence, save for the chopping of their knives and sizzle of sautéing butter. Soon the kitchen was filled with the aroma of roasting turkey, butter, mushrooms, and a host of other scents.

Paul had never cooked with her. It was almost as if with Paul they were living two separate lives within one household. She liked this companionship with Theodore. It felt, already, like some sort of partnership.

"What's next?" he asked her, finishing the prep for the stuffed mushrooms.

"Well, we have chips and French onion dip, so that sour cream needs to be mixed with that envelope. That's the Midwestern side. And then the foodie side needs chopped artichokes and Parmesan and a few other things."

"I can do both," Theodore said. On his way to grab the sour cream, he paused, drew Dana into a hug and kissed her. "Thank you," he said again.

"You've already thanked me. You don't have to keep doing it. I'm glad you're here."

"I don't just mean for Thanksgiving. I mean for all of it. For allowing me to be here…in your life."

Dana held a chocolate covered spoon out to him, the spoon she'd been using to stir the frosting for a chocolate torte with. "Do not say that again or I'm liable to cry. And tears and chocolate don't mix. I'm sure there's a song somewhere that says exactly that."

In response, he kissed her again.

Chapter 67

By noon, all the side dishes were prepped and ready to go. The chocolate torte was frosted and encircled with raspberries. The turkey made the house smell warm and buttery and…like a home.

Theodore liked the cozy feel of the place. He liked the smell of the kitchen, the kids watching TV in the other room. He liked watching Dana hop through the kitchen, trying to navigate. He liked her green cast. He didn't want to go back to his cold apartment. Not now. Not ever.

"Dana," he said. She was filling bowls with assorted dips and did not turn to him. "Dana," he said again.

"Huh?" She looked up at him. She had a smear of dip above her eyebrow.

Theodore thought it was quite possibly the cutest thing he'd ever seen. "You know in Las Vegas when Elvis asked me if I'd promise to love you tender and take care of you in my blue suede shoes?"

"Yes?" she said, her voice sounding like a question.

"I want to promise that again. Only maybe not with Elvis asking me, but a clergyman or priest or whoever marries people. Because that's what I want. I want to marry you. I know it's fast, but I've never been so sure of anything in my life. And if you want me to get down on my knees, I will. In fact, I want to." He lowered himself to his knees.

Suddenly, they heard the kids' footsteps. "What are you doing, Theo?" asked Ruby. "Why are you on the floor? Did you lose something?"

"No, Ruby. Not exactly." He was kneeling now and turned to face the kids. "I was asking your mom to marry me. Is that okay with you?"

Zach said, "It's okay with me. But she's the one that's gotta say yes. What do you say, Mom?"

"It's a little quick," she began.

Ruby said, "You're always telling me I'm fast and that I do a good job."

"That's true," she said.

Theodore spun on his knee and faced her again. "I mean it, Dana. I'm in love with you and now that I've found you, I don't really want to pretend that I haven't. I don't want to take extra time just because others might think we should. Maybe it's rushing it, but I don't care. I want you in my life, and I want to be in your life and your kids' life. If the kids will let me, I'll love them too and be a good stepdad. I can't promise I'll be perfect, but I promise to try, and to never hurt you and to try to give you what you need. I'm crazy about you."

"Say yes, Mom!" Ruby shouted.

"Do it for the Federation, Mom!" Zach said.

"Say yes, only if you want to," Theodore said.

Dana didn't say yes. She shouted it.

Chapter 68

Dana wasn't quite sure when it happened, but it was after her parents arrived, and after Valerie and Vick got into a fight, and after one of the twins projectile vomited all over the pumpkin pie, that someone got the bright idea that they should rent a van and go to Vegas and finish what Dana and Theodore had started.

She wasn't even entirely sure that she had told them that crazy or not, Theodore had proposed to her, and she'd screamed yes. Somehow, just by looking at her, they knew.

"Don't worry," Valerie said. "The twins aren't sick. They're like puppies. They'll eat until they explode. Usually, I cut them off before they reach that point, but I was distracted by that chocolate torte. We can totally do a wedding after we clean them up."

Dana nodded. She didn't remember actually agreeing to the crazy scheme, but somehow Theodore and her father had taken off to find a rental car; they'd have to go to the only open store, which was located near the airport in Grand Rapids. With the van, the whole family could be in Vegas in just three short days. Or quite possibly three of the longest days ever, if she stopped to imagine what the car ride would be like.

"Valerie! Why did I agree to this! This is crazy!" Dana said, shaking her head.

"Which part?" Valerie asked.

"All of it. Sending Dad off with Theodore, for one. I mean, I shouldn't have let Dad get him alone. He's going to fill his head with all sorts of weirdness. And the Vegas trip? Valerie, that's three days in a van. With our family. And kids. This isn't bright. In fact, it's downright suicidal."

"Well, if that's all that's wrong, we can deal with that. You didn't mention the marrying part."

Dana paused. "Funny thing is, I actually want to do that. And as quickly as possible."

"Is he that good?" Valerie asked, lowering her voice so Ruby in the next room couldn't hear. "You know…does he make sweet love to you. Although, I'm not sure anyone makes sweet love, except in songs. And maybe erotica novels."

"We haven't even done it yet. There have been," Dana paused, wondering how to phrase it, "complications. And not just my foot."

"Can't he get it up?"

"Of course he can! I just meant that I didn't want to, you know, with the kids in the house."

Valerie just looked at her. "Dana, you're thirty-seven. Let me tell you, a hushed quickie in the basement or your bedroom is probably all you're going to get for a while. This is called sex in your middle age. Or at least sex while being a parent. I've had sex *while* folding laundry."

"No!"

"It's true. I mean, I have a To Do list. Sometimes I multi-task."

Dana laughed. There was some truth to it. At the same time, it wasn't all bad. She'd sorta like to have sex with Theodore while folding laundry. It sounded dangerous.

"Still, travelling to Vegas is kind of ridiculous. And Theodore needs to get back to his store. There must be something else we can do."

"How about we let the men figure that out? It will puff them full of Testosterone," Dana's mom said.

Both Dana and Valerie jumped. They hadn't even known she'd been standing there. She had a way of doing that. She'd stealthily sneak up on you and start giving you a backrub. Backrubs were nice, but a bit freaky if you weren't expecting one.

"I'll text them and let them know they need to come up with Plan B." Dana's mom grabbed her phone and went into the living room.

Dana said, "I'm not sure which part of that statement is more disturbing. That Mom clearly heard what we were talking about and seems to have no reaction, or that she's actually figured out how to text."

Valerie agreed. "Come on," she said. "Let's go look in your closet for something to wear. We have maybe forty more minutes to plan you a wedding. I'm taking over as the event planner. It's good practice for me. Vick!" she called. They heard Vick before they saw him. He had a twin on each hip, and Zach and Ruby were both attached to one leg.

"We're playing monster," he offered.

"Whatever," Valerie said. "Just keep them occupied. We've got packing to do. And maybe clean up a little if you can."

Chapter 69

Theodore was starting to freak out a little bit. Not because he had just planned to marry Dana and as quickly as possible, but because her father was delivering a thirty-minute monologue that belonged in a Tarantino film. It was rife with action and blood and weird cultural references and something about his fascination with cheeseburgers done on a real grill, not a gas grill.

"The charcoal is key. You don't have a good burger without a little carcinogen. You know what I mean?"

With that, they pulled out of the Gerald Ford International Airport in their newly rented white van. "I do know what you mean. And I promise that once I marry your daughter I will never use a gas grill again."

"That's good. That's what I want to hear. Because if you do and I find out about it, well, there were things we used to do in the Guard. Bad things. Let's just say there were punishments that involved duct tape and the hair on your butt. Everyone's got hair on their butt. You don't realize it until it's been ripped off."

Theodore gulped. He must really want to marry Dana or this guy would terrify him. As it was, he was mildly amused.

Ralph's phone chimed. "That's a message," he said. "Will you check that out? I don't like to do it while I'm driving. I mean, I could, of course, I'm trained for that sort of thing, but it's illegal here in Michigan. You know that, right?"

"Yes, Sir," Theodore agreed. He grabbed the phone. "It's from your wife. She says…" Theodore silently read. "She says maybe Las Vegas is ambitious and isn't there anything closer."

Ralph grunted and slapped the steering wheel. "You must really have my daughter wrapped up in a love blanket. She wants you. What do you say to that? Do you know of anywhere closer? And are you going to call your family and let them know this scheme you're planning on pulling off?"

Theodore was suddenly overwhelmed with thoughts. Why were they doing this so quickly? Sarah had been planning their wedding for years, even before they were engaged, probably even before they met. How did he think he could pull this off in less than twenty-four hours? Still. He wanted to marry Dana. And he wanted to do it now.

Crazy, impulsive actions weren't necessarily natural to him, but he saw no reason to wait. Theodore could see his new life with Dana and the kids just in front of him, and he didn't want to wait for it. He wanted to start on that life now.

Finally, an idea came to him. "I don't know of any place closer, but let me make a call. And then, yeah, I'll let my family know." Theodore and Dana had pretended to get married in Vegas, but there was something to what Ralph said. This time, Theodore wanted to do this the right way, even if it was spur-of-the-moment, and he wanted his family with him. And his family included his parents, and Mike, and now the woman he was calling.

"Hello, Angelique?" he began. Strange. It was as if she was expecting his call.

Chapter 70

"Okay, remind me of why you got married in the first time. Not to Paul, but to, you know, Theodore. In Vegas."

"I don't want to tell you. It's too embarrassing."

Valerie poked her head out of the closet. "You've seen me completely naked and were in the delivery room when I birthed those babies. I think I'm owed some embarrassing stories from you."

Dana shrugged. "Okay. I was dressed as a 1980s rocker. Like, uh, Madonna."

"What? With the crosses and jelly bracelets?"

"And the big hair."

Valerie went back into the closet. "I can see why they suggest that you shouldn't talk about what happens in Vegas. That's so embarrassing!"

"Valerie!" Dana said, with a half-laugh. "And, yes, I still have the outfit. It's tucked in the back of the closet, but I don't think I really want to wear it."

"Never fear," Valerie said, emerging with a green floral dress that Dana had bought a few months ago at a vintage store. It was a spur of the moment purchase, and she never really thought she'd wear it. "You are going to wear this. And you're going to look amazing. Like a 1950s starlet."

"I'm too old to be a starlet," Dana said, reaching out to touch the fabric. It was a lovely dress with crinoline and a flared dress that fit tight around the waist and little cap sleeves.

"You might be too old to be a starlet, true," Valerie conceded. "But you're never too old to be a pinup. And you, my darling sister, will be so hot in this. I swear, you should've been born in the fifties. But I'm glad you weren't, because then you probably would've dated Dad."

"Ew."

Valerie handed her the dress. "Try it on."

Chapter 71

Ralph pulled into Theodore's driveway so that he could pick up something to wear. "Pick something comfortable," he said to Theodore. "I got married in a tuxedo. Dumbest thing I've ever done. Everyone kept mistaking me for a waiter."

"Why don't you come on in, Ralph?" Theodore said when it looked like Ralph had planned to keep the motor running. "You can give me some pointers."

Angelique had been ecstatic when Theodore called and assured him she knew exactly where to go and who could marry them. She just had to make a few phone calls first. Then she'd tell them where they could all rendezvous.

"I'm glad you're listening to your heart about that woman. She's good for you," Angelique had said. And Theodore had agreed.

"I'll take care of everything," Angelique had continued. "I'll call Mike and your parents too if you want. They're in Florida, right? So getting them here could prove tricky. I'll handle it. You just focus on getting something nice to wear and picking up your bride-to-be and her kids, and maybe pack up those leftovers so we can have a party afterwards." Theodore had readily agreed.

Now, he was in his house, heading up to his closet to do exactly as Angelique had instructed. Just as he was about to begin rifling through his closet, he felt Ralph's hand on his shoulder.

"Let me do this, son," he said. "It may surprise you, but I know a thing or two about fashion. And about what will look good standing next to my daughter."

How could Theodore argue with that?

Chapter 72

The dress was perfect. It fit her curves and fell to just below the knees. Her legs would have been very shapely if one of them weren't encased in the gigantic green cast.

"I think this is fate," Valerie said. "Even the cast matches. It's all like it was preordained or something. Is that the right word? That sounds religious."

"I think it's the right word. It doesn't matter. This is what I'm wearing. Now we just need something for Zach and Ruby."

"Have you talked to them about this?" Valerie asked gently.

Dana scrunched her face. Had she? She'd been so caught up in the moment that she really hadn't thought to explain in detail what was happening. The kids were there when Theodore had proposed, but did they fully understand what that meant? She had a moment of panic followed by a sort of warming. It was just like her mother said. Sometimes you just know.

"Why don't you pick them out something?" she said to Valerie. "I want to just talk to them one more time first."

Dana used her crutches to get to the stairs then sat and slowly moved her way down, bumping gently on her bottom all the way. What if when she explained how their lives would change because of this, what if the kids told her not to do it? Could she give up this fantasy for herself? Would she be forced to?

She tried not to think about it because she already knew the answer. She would do whatever was required to keep her kids happy, even if that meant living alone.

Chapter 73

Ralph handed Theodore an outfit. "It's perfect," he said.

Theodore agreed.

"Well," he continued with a slap on Theodore's back, "I don't have to tell you that if you break her heart or the kids', I'll kill ya. I know a thousand different ways to do it. Trained in Special Forces in the National Guard, Michigan Division. I could torture you with nothing but a toothpick and the will of God. But I don't need to tell you that, do I?"

Theodore didn't say anything. He couldn't. He couldn't breathe.

"Aw, come here," Ralph said and gathered him into a warm embrace. "I'm tickled pink. Pink! Just don't let that get out."

"Yes, sir," Theodore said.

"All right then. Let's get this show on the road. Are you ready for this?"

Theodore knew that Ralph was asking him more than if he was just ready to head to Coopersville. He wanted to know if he was really ready to commit to Dana and to her children, to sharing a life with her, to growing old with her.

"A hundred percent," he said.

Ralph seemed to study him. "In the Guard, we'd say a hundred and ten percent. But I can work on you."

Chapter 74

Dana clomped into the living room. "Kids," she said gently. Ruby and Zach looked up. They'd been scaring the twins with monster faces, which the twins adored. "I need to talk to you."

"What did we do?" Zach said. "They like it when we scare them."

"I know, I know, it's just…come over here and talk to Mommy, okay? Let Uncle Vick hang out with his sons for a bit."

The kids followed her into the kitchen.

She awkwardly lowered herself onto the floor, casted leg extended so they could sit in her lap. "Come here," she said. Maybe the kids knew she was serious because they didn't squirm or fuss or bite each other. Ruby snuggled against one side of her and Zach took the other.

"You know how Theodore asked if he could marry me?"

"Yeah," they said in unison.

"I want to make sure before I do this that this is okay with both of you. It's important to me that you guys want this. That you like Theodore. I don't expect you to love him right away, that will take time, but I want you involved in the decision. Okay?" The kids didn't say anything. Dana could feel her heart in her chest. Did this mean they didn't want her to?

After a moment, Ruby said, "Mom, my butt hurts. I don't want to sit on the ground anymore. Can we get up?"

"Yes, but you haven't answered the question. Is it okay if Mommy marries Theodore?"

Zach harrumphed. "I thought we already went through this. We love Theo, Mom. He just feels like he sort of fits here, right? This one's up to you. Do *you* want to marry him?"

Dana felt tears in her eyes and she squeezed her kids close to her. "Oh, yes," she said.

"Then can we please just do it so that we don't have to wait anymore? We're only kids, Mom. We don't have a lot of patience."

"Yeah," Ruby agreed.

Just then, they heard the happy beeping of a rented van's horn as it pulled into the driveway.

Chapter 75

A half hour later, they were all on their way to Saugatuck, Michigan, about an hour's drive away and located on the shore of Lake Michigan. Angelique had given Theodore instructions, and they loaded the van with all the leftover turkey fixings they could. They also had suitcases packed with wedding clothes. In the van, they were all seated. Ralph drove and Dana sat in the front seat where she was most comfortable with her leg. Zach and Ruby sat in the next row with a baby between them, followed by Valerie, Vick and another baby. Theodore sat in the back with Dana's mother.

"There's no escaping now," she warned him.

"It's okay, Mrs. Kupiac," Theodore said.

"Mrs. Kupiac. Hmmm. In another few hours, why don't you just call me Mom?"

Theodore agreed to that too.

And then with the revving of the van's engine and Meatloaf blaring on the CD player, they were off. Heading towards the future.

Chapter 76

"Where are we?" Dana asked.

They'd driven into downtown Saugatuck with its Victorian houses, close streets, and a main street that was, without question, quaint.

"We're supposed to go to the Little Playhouse which is… Oh," Dana asked just as Theodore pointed to the marquee above him. In lights were the words DANA AND THEO GET HITCHED. It was an old-fashioned movie theater, which was now used mostly for cabaret acts to entertain the tourists.

It hit Dana squarely in the stomach. They were going to do this. They were going to get married, and not for pretend this time, but for real. And they were doing it now. Theo parked the van and turned it off.

"Theo?" Dana asked quietly.

He walked over to her as their group grabbed all the stuff from the car. He took her hand.

"Are you sure about this?" she asked. "Because you can back out now. It's okay. We can think more about this later if we want. We don't have to do this now. It's sort of ridiculous. It could possibly be even foolish or at least dangerous."

"I'm sure," he said without hesitating. "Dana, you're the woman I want to spend my life with, and I want to share it with you and the kids. We can pretend we don't know that and postpone it until it's socially acceptable, but I really want to stop living my life for the future. I'm ready to live in the now. And I want you. Now." He leaned over and kissed her.

"Keep it down over there. Wait until you say your I Do's," Dana's dad called out.

Dana couldn't help but laugh. This was turning out to be the strangest Thanksgiving she'd ever experienced, and certainly one she'd be grateful for.

"Okay, then," she said. "Let's get everything inside. We're getting married in less than an hour."

Chapter 77

Angelique stood in the center of the stage, waiting for them as they walked in. "What do you think, Theodore?" she asked, opening her arms and motioning to the stage that was decorated with flowers. "Not bad for just a couple of hours notice, is it?"

Theodore couldn't believe his eyes. There were flowers everywhere. "How did you manage this?"

"Honey, I am connected. These come from the show that just closed here. Not only am I a business whiz, but I'm also a singer. I perform here on occasion. Not only that…" she said with a wide grin. "I'm also a minister."

"You're kidding, right?" Theodore walked on stage and gave her a hug. "Not that I doubt you."

"Well, I'm not the religious kind of minister. Let's just say I have friends who want to get married, and I, on occasion, perform the ceremony. All you need is a little online certificate, which I have. So don't worry. What we're going to do here will be entirely legal. And permanent. You got that?"

Theodore nodded.

"Good. Now introduce me to your fiancée. We have a wedding to throw."

Chapter 78

This was crazy. Utterly crazy! And wickedly fun. Dana was having the time of her life. Angelique had led them to a room in the back of the theater where actors usually got dressed. The dressing room was lined with mirrors and lights. Ruby wore her red tutu over a pair of jeans and had on a purple turtleneck. She also wore a crown.

"Mom! Watch me spin!" She spun once, wobbled, nearly fell over, but caught her balance.

Zach was in his Clone Trooper outfit, complete with mask and light saber. He was practicing the Jedi moves he'd use as they walked down the aisle. "Not all Jedis can walk and do their moves at the same time, but I can," he said.

"You're very gifted," Dana's mother said. She had just finished pinning an antique brooch to Dana's dress. "It was your Great Aunt Maddie's. She was the flapper in our family, remember? She's the one that was married to a seventy-five year old when she was twenty, so she could get his money and then she ended up eloping with the milkman. Smart lady. It seemed appropriate."

"What else does she need?" Valerie asked.

"Something old, something new, something borrowed, something blue," her mother chanted. "Your dress is old. So, check."

"It's vintage," Dana corrected.

"But the rhyme doesn't say vintage. In the rhyme it says old. And you can borrow the brooch. You can have it back when I'm dead. Valerie, I have a ring for you." Dana and Valerie didn't have a chance to respond to that. Their mother just kept talking. Dana knew it was probably a combination of excitement and anxiety. "Something new…"

"I've got that!" Valerie said, reaching for her purse. "It's supposed to be your Christmas present, but shoot. Have it now." She handed her a little box.

Inside was a necklace with a bird on it; attached to it was a tag that read: *Faith is believing in one of two things: that there will be something for you to stand on, or you will be taught to fly.* "I know it's a little cheesy but I sorta think that maybe this year with the divorce and your broken foot, maybe you were just learning to fly." Valerie kissed Dana's cheek and then fastened the necklace around her neck.

"And now for something blue!" Dana's mom said. She leaned in and whispered into Dana's ear while slipping something into her palm, "It's another condom. It's in a blue wrapper. Slip it into your cast. You can use it later. Unless, you know, you two want to have more babies."

Chapter 79

Theodore, Mike, Mike's girlfriend Mavis, and Dana's dad Ralph, were in the Green Room.

"You look stunning," Mavis said.

Theodore could see, at least initially, what drew Mike to Mavis. She was in her late-fifties, true, but there was a quiet elegance and sensuality to her, sort of like Helen Mirren the actress. And around her, Mike seemed incredibly calm and not as much as an asshole. Maybe Mavis brought out the best in him.

"I like the shirt," Mike said.

"Ralph picked it out." It was a blue Hawaiian shirt with white flowers. At first, Theodore had been hesitant, but then he'd quickly agreed. Getting married shouldn't just be a show, it should also somehow be a reflection of your personality joining with another. In Sarah's plans, she had Theodore wearing a tuxedo along with a dozen groomsmen, most of whom he didn't know. Theodore had felt he was just a stand-in for someone else's role. Now, though, he felt like the principal actor. All of which made getting married in a theater seem most appropriate.

"I think I'm ready," Theodore said.

"You think?" Ralph boomed. "You think? There's no thinking for you anymore, son. After today, you do exactly what Dana tells you, and you will have a very comfortable life. It's what I do. My wife, she's the boss." Ralph smiled, his tough guy act disintegrating. "I sure am happy to have you in the family," he finished, and Theodore thought he saw tears in the older man's eyes.

The door opened and they smelled cinnamon and patchouli.

"Get out here," Angelique said, "We are ready to go."

Chapter 80

It was amazing what Angelique had come up with in just a few hours. "I called in a few favors," she said, quickly followed by, "and you owe me."

The theater was dark except for the illuminated stage. They'd put chairs on the stage so that everyone would be a part of the ceremony. Mike and Mavis sat together, next to Dana's hipster friends Jennie and Brent. And there was a laptop sitting open on a stool.

"What on earth?" Theodore said.

"Check it out," Angelique said. "We're Skyping the wedding."

Theodore looked at the computer screen, where his parents, golden from the Florida sun waved at him. "Hello, Theodore!" his mother chimed. "So happy for you and this new woman. Can't wait to meet her!"

"We never liked Sarah," his father said. "I'm sorry, but it's true."

"She was too controlling," his mother agreed. "We love that we can be there with you. Oh! And look who else can join us!" His mother held up a little white dog. "Isn't she cute?"

"Her name is Killer," his dad said. "Enjoy the day, son. We do wish we could be there."

Theodore was beyond words.

"Okay, Theodore, you stand right there and just wait. Your part is easy," Angelique said. "Oh, and I have one more surprise for you. Okay, fellas!" she called.

Theodore hadn't noticed the risers on the stage, but now, now they were being filled by a group of men wearing bad holiday sweaters.

"It's the Saugatuck Gay Men's Chorus. I also conduct a little music on the side," Angelique said. "Is everyone ready?"

The chorus hooted and said a variety of things like "Oh, yes!" and "Do it!"

"You ready?" Angelique asked.

"You bet," Theodore answered, and he meant it with every fiber of his being. With that, Angelique's wife played the opening chords to "Love Me Tender" and the chorus began to sing.

Chapter 81

Dana stood with her family outside the theater. Vick walked in first with the twins. They hadn't really planned anything; it was just happening. Dana felt as if she sort of floated outside herself. At the same time, she knew she was doing exactly what she ought to do. Her mom and dad kissed her and then walked inside.

"You ready for this?" Valerie asked. "Because you can turn back if you want to. We'll judge you, but we'll get over it."

Dana laughed. "No. This is right, Val. It really is."

"I think so too," Valerie said and touched her forehead to Dana's. "I love you, sister."

"I love you, too."

"Okay, kiddos, you follow me, okay?" Valerie said. She walked into the auditorium, followed by a twirling and leaping Ruby and Zach, who attacked imaginary evil Jedi fighters all down the aisle.

Dana took a deep breath. A year ago she'd been broken and thought she'd never laugh or love again. And now, now, her heart felt bigger than ever. She might still be broken, but at least it was just her foot. That would heal. Just like over the last year her heart had. Sometimes being foolish and rushing into something fell more like following the swift arc of a wish.

She listened to the male chorus's simple harmonies, and even though she walked slowly onward with the use of her crutches, she felt as if she flew down the aisle toward the man and the future that waited for her.

Chapter 82

Dana was sure that years from now, she would look back on that day and laugh. She waited at the bottom of the stage until the chorus was done singing and then, with the help of Ruby holding up her dress and flashing the empty auditorium, Dana crawled up the steps. It was actually easier and probably safer than having someone lift her, and for some reason, Dana wanted to reach Theo on her own.

Zach handed her the crutches, and Dana clomped forward to meet Theodore.

"I'm not going to spend a lot of time talking to you," Angelique said. "It seems obvious that you two are in a hurry to get on with your lives, now that you found each other. I, for one, believe that's the way it is when you meet your soul mate. It's comfortable. It's like meeting an old friend. And you just know that things are going to work out. Dana and Theodore, your friends and family know you are going to work out. Your love radiates off of you and wraps all of us a little bit closer. So let's do this, okay? Let's make this wedding official."

Dana handed Valerie her crutches and hopped over to Theo. He wrapped his arm around her waist, and she felt supported, literally and emotionally.

Angelique continued, "Do you, Theodore Drimmel, promise to love Dana Kupiac and her children as they are a package deal? Do you promise to treat them with kindness and fairness and to listen to them? Do you promise to respect Dana both as your wife and as the individual and wonderful woman that she is? Do you promise to love her authentically, truthfully, and with your whole being for as long as you both shall live?"

"I do," he said.

"And do you, Dana, promise to keep your heart open and love Theodore and appreciate him and support him as long as you both shall live?"

"Is that it?" Dana asked.

"I've found women need less instruction than the men," Angelique confirmed.

"With all my heart, I do." Dana agreed.

Angelique turned to Ruby and Zach who, miraculously, were not fighting with each other. "And do you Ruby and Zach promise to treat your new stepdad with respect and love and kindness?"

Zach looked at his feet. "I'm six," he said.

Ruby chimed in and said, "I'm four-an-a-half!"

Angelique nodded. "I hear you. You can't be perfect all the time. You're kids. But do you promise to try?"

"I promise!" they said.

At that point everyone, even the chorus, was crying. No one even heard Angelique say, "I now pronounce you husband and wife!" because amidst the crying there were also cheers.

Chapter 83

That night, Dana and Theodore registered at the JW in downtown Grand Rapids. The hotel was located on the Grand River and boasted a view of the city awash in light. It was well past midnight now, and even though they were tired, they were also exited. They'd rented two adjoining rooms on a lower floor for Dana's parents and the kids, and they'd made sure the kids were tucked in bed, and her parents were comfortable with watching them before heading up to their own room.

The day, the night, the last few months even, everything had been a whirlwind of laughter and fun and even a little romance. First they'd had the dream of Las Vegas; now it seemed like they'd never wake up. After they said their vows, everyone helped clear the stage and brought in leftovers from the afternoon Thanksgiving. Then word must have gotten out in Saugatuck that there was a party going on because people just started showing up. It seemed everyone was bored with their own families and just started arriving. They carried wine and spiked eggnog, leftover turkey, sweet potatoes, mashed potatoes, pie. Some brought caviar and crackers. It was, indeed, a foodie's delight.

Someone started playing music on the loudspeaker and Dana and Theodore along with the kiddos danced. Of course, Dana couldn't move very well with her foot, but she felt as if she was dancing anyway.

And for their slow dance, Theodore simply held her close. "I love you, you know. I don't know why or how all of this happened, but I'm glad it did."

"I'm glad, too," she said, and then kissed him, telling him everything she felt for him without needing to say a word.

Finally, when Ruby and Zach fell asleep, and Valerie and Vick cradled their sleeping twins close to them, they decided to call it a night. Angelique and her wife, along with Mike and Mavis, Jennie and Brent, took care of clean up and Theodore promised that even though he was having an impromptu honeymoon night, he would be at Foodies bright and early for Black Friday. Only this time, Dana would go with him. She'd run the cash register. They already had a plan to work on distribution of her jams and jellies, which Valerie would head. They were going to make Foodies a national chain, but first they'd start small. They just had big plans.

Theo pressed the up button on the elevator. "You look incredibly sexy in that dress," he said, and then he kissed the side of her neck. "And that cast…wow."

"Just be glad I'm wearing a dress," Dana said. "Yesterday. I actually got stuck in my pants and had to cut them off. If I'm wearing any pants for the next six weeks, they're going to be yoga pants."

"Whatever you wear is great. Even if it's just the cast." He paused. "Especially if it's just the cast."

The elevator dinged and they walked in. Theodore made sure the door didn't close as Dana navigated the threshold with her crutches.

Once the elevator closed, Theo pulled her to him. "I think on some level, even in Las Vegas, I knew we'd end up here."

"In an elevator again? Are we going to make out?" Dana asked.

"Yes. We are. But that's not just what I mean. I mean, I think what happened in Vegas was just a preview. We're going to have a lot of fun together." Theo kissed her forehead gently.

Dana could already feel her temperature rising. "Well, I'm glad that what happened in Vegas didn't stay in Vegas. I'm glad you found me."

"I was lost without you. Granted, I didn't know it, but I'm glad we found each other."

"Can we stop talking now?" Dana asked. The elevator dinged and the doors opened to their floor.

Theodore leaned over and pressed several buttons. One on the top floor, one on the bottom, and a few in between. They could stay in the elevator all night if they wanted, though she knew they wouldn't.

"Yes, please," he said. Then he drew her to him and they kissed.

They kissed like new lovers, and teenagers, and soul mates. They kissed like old friends, and a couple in their mid-thirties. They kissed like they were in love, because they were, and they knew that somehow whatever crazy misadventures awaited them in the future, they'd be able to face it together.

In the elevator, Dana even bent her casted leg, the way a woman in photos does when she's getting a good kiss, and Theo dipped her, proving, that maybe, just maybe you could be an awkward foodie and still end up incredibly lucky.

Acknowledgments

I just want to take a couple of moments to formally thank some very cool ladies. For my sister Heidi Ogle, you are one tough dame and I love you for your strength and support. You inspired Valerie, though thankfully, you never talk as much about your nipples as she does about hers.

And for my friends Laura Michels and Dana Harrison. Laura, I've loved our walk-therapy. I'll have to put something like that in future books. Dana Harrison: thank you for believing in my work. You asked that if I used your name, that the character at least be able to cook.

"Foodies Rush In" was written for National Novel Writing Month in November 2010. The goal was to write 1,667 words a day so that by the end of the month, you have a 50,000 word novel. I decided to give it a try. I'd participate in the 2009 NaNoWriMo and came up with some material for my third book "Pepper Wellington and the Case of the Missing Sausage". So, even though November is a busy month with the beginning of the holidays, I sat down every day and wrote my 1,667 words.

To make it happen, I had to wake up at 5:00 or 5:30 in the morning, slightly before the kids. Sometimes, the kids woke up before, and I'd make them breakfast and they'd watch a program while I wrote. We agreed it was only for the month of November. They didn't seem to mind. On days when I didn't have the kids, I still woke up early in the morning. It felt good to start the day off writing.

This book symbolizes a new turn in not just my writing but my life. Like Dana, as a single mom, I thought love wasn't possible. Or finding a man who would be good to me and for me and the kiddos was a fantasy. I'm glad to say I've been proven wrong. This book, then is for David, who has taught me that love can come from the most unlikely source, even if that source is looking you right in the eye, sitting on your porch and drinking a Mai Tai. David and I knew each other for years before dating; in fact, I dated a good friend of his. It's how we met.

So I wanted to write a story where love happens naturally. I didn't want there to be something separating the main characters from their love. I wanted the story to be about them finally finding each other.

I guess because that's what I feel has happened in my own life. So, for all the people out there who are lonely and still looking, have faith. It will happen.

Cheers,

Tanya

About The Author

Tanya Eby is the author of "Blunder Woman", "Easy Does It", and "Pepper Wellington and the Case of the Missing Sausage". She lives in Grand Rapids, Michigan with her tiki-obsessed husband and two quirky children. Please visit her blog at **tanyaeby.com**.